# Dragon's Gambit

## Chloe Knight

*To my sister Stephanie, who started this series by asking me to write a science fiction story, and to my mother who has been my biggest supporter*

# Chapter One

The interrogation room reeked of flowers and fresh dirt. There was not a single smudge on the white walls, or visible dirt on the white carpet, not even near the potted plants. The table I was chained to was polished to a radiant shine, and even the chains couldn't scratch it – I tried.

It wasn't the chains that bothered me, prisoners were often restrained, that was nothing new, what bothered was the pristine white carpet. It was a false sense of security, to make the prisoner think nothing violent would happen here, because there was no evidence that anything violent *had* happened on this carpet. However, it was equally clear to see the carpet was new, so all it truly meant was that these people had the resources to replace the carpet often, possibly after each interrogation.

The interrogator, a bored, portly man with a thick head of hair and perfectly fitting uniform of crisp gold and black fabric, stepped into the room, reading a screen as he walked to the table and sat down. Whatever was on the screen was apparently more interesting than me, I wasn't even worth a glance.

I considered thinning the mental wall I kept around my power. I was a telepath, capable of reading emotions, memories, and even on occasion thoughts. But there was a dark side to my power, a temptation. I could manipulate the emotions I read, it was so effortless, and oh, so addicting. To ensure I didn't manipulate every person I came across, I maintained the mental wall that sealed away my power and gave the added benefit of ensuring no other telepath could read my thoughts or emotions. If I lowered it, another telepath could read my thoughts and emotions. Or, more dangerously, I could manipulate the guard too much, go too far and turn him into my own personal puppet.

For now, the risks were too great, I would simply have to wait and see how this played out.

"State your name," he said woodenly, his gaze still focused on the screen.

"Taya of the City of Brookfield," I said with a calmness I didn't feel. It wasn't my real name, it wasn't close to my real name, but it was the name on my file.

"Brookfield, that's on Terra 9, right? Isn't that the planet that had that devastating volcanic eruption? Did you live on the ocean side or the desert side of Brookfield?"

"The Desert side," I said promptly. Most planets had their wealthy live near water, and I was attempting to pass as a nobody, unworthy of the attention of this man.

"Ah, that's interesting. See, I'm originally from Terra 9. My aunt lived in Brookfield. It's in the middle of a forest as far from deserts and oceans as you can get," he said in an idle, conversational tone, his focus back on that cursed screen.

I didn't respond. I knew refugees from Terra 9 came to this world, but I would have never guessed that my interrogator was one. The refugees left with nothing, forced to start over on new worlds with new cultures and expectations. This man either had connections on this world, or luck, to get such a good job.

He looked at me, his focus finally away from the screen. "Do you want to try again? What is your name? Where are you from, truly?"

"My name is Taya," I said quietly.

He shook his head and pulled a small metal disk out of his pocket. He released it into the air. It spun towards me and zipped around my jacket. In seconds, my jacket was nothing but shreds of cloth on the table and floor. That nasty little thing didn't shred my tank top, fortunately, or the baggy, stained slacks I wore.

"The tattoo on your bicep, the flame in the circle? That's the symbol of one of Setne's Hunters from the planet Nexa. Are you a spy? You clearly aren't a particularly good one."

I glanced at my arm. That tattoo was only one of the reasons I always wore long sleeves. I tried to twist so the tattoo wasn't visible. As soon as I realized it was futile, I relaxed and sat up straight.

Never show how they hurt you.

When I didn't respond, the interrogator continued.

"Your file flagged when you stepped off the refugee ship. It was a simple thing at first, until the DNA scan came back, but the first thing that flagged was your natural hair color listed as black on your file. I guess those checkpoint delays took far longer than you anticipated, and you had no access to hair dye? There is a reason the instructions state to put your natural hair and eye color.'"

"I'm not a spy, I'm a refugee," I said, ignoring the statement about my hair color. The truth was, I hadn't realized it would be so important. My file was forged without my input, and even if they had asked, I would have given black as my natural color. However, after over a year of travel, my natural hair, brown streaked with white, had grown out, leaving faded black tips. Since I didn't think explaining that I wasn't involved in the forgery of my paperwork would help my case, I tried another tactic.

"I would like to formally request asylum on Karabeeya, in the Kingdom of Valoria."

"And those are the magic words," he said with a smirk. "A Nexa Hunter asking for asylum in the capital of Valoria." He stood up and picked up his screen, his attention once again on whatever information he was reading. Without another word or any further explanation, he walked out of the room and the door shut quickly behind him.

I was once again left in the room, alone.

Time was irrelevant in the brightly lit, silent room, and I

was not good with boredom. I even contemplated using my other power, although that would blow up any possibility, I had at being accepted as a refugee here, both literally and figuratively.

Since I couldn't blow anything up, or risk annoying my captors by singing obscene songs, another tempting possibility, I moved the chains around and settled my head on my hands and took a nap. The mental wall I maintained took a lot of magic, and the best way to replenish magic was with sleep. I was a master at falling asleep anywhere.

I had just settled into the deep sleep, the one past boredom and restlessness and into true relaxation, when a loud thud echoed through the room and rudely interrupted my nap. I snapped up from the table and squinted with annoyance at the interrogator. There were plenty of ways he could have woken me up without doing it by slamming the door closed.

"You were actually taking a nap?" he demanded incredulously.

"I was bored. What do you do when you're bored?" I snapped before I caught myself. My life and future relied on not annoying this guy into sending me back to Nexa or throwing me in some cell and forgetting I existed.

"Put your hands flat on the table," he ordered.

I did what he demanded, and he unlocked the chain from the table.

"Stand up, and don't put of a fight. The king has granted you an audience. It's not something he often does for refugees requesting asylum but yours is a special case."

"What do you mean?" I asked. I assumed it was because I was a former Nexa Hunter and possibly the first to ask for asylum in this king's country, but I learned a long time ago to never assume. He didn't respond, few of my questions had been answered since I was pulled from the refugee line and had these chains snapped on my wrists and feet.

I knew a little about this world, Karabeeya. It had three kingdoms, two were ruled by kings, the third by something called an Eoness, which was probably like a king. Unfortunately, I did not know much about the customs or cultures of the kingdoms, or even the names of the rulers. I didn't think knowing that information was important. The refugees from my ship were to be hired to work in the swamps after a plague ravaged the lower class, and no one else was willing to do such menial labor.

He led me into the hallway where four other guards were waiting. I wasn't sure how well they could stop me if I wanted to escape, and out of habit, I considered my options. A small explosion to break the chains, then I risked getting shot by the guards. There was no straightforward way out of this except with using my telepathy to manipulate them into letting me escape with minimal effort, and I wasn't ready to risk the fallout from that. Instead, I walked in the center of their ring, down an empty hallway, and through two sets of doors.

The second set of doors led us to a large, circular room with murals of heroic soldiers in the same uniform as those who surrounded me. I wasn't sure if they were guards, soldiers, or this area's law enforcement. I didn't ask.

They stopped in front of a set of gold doors and waited until they opened to reveal a small room, an elevator. The elevator was another example of the wealth in this building. Every wall was carved with images of marine life unlike anything I had ever seen before, although the creatures were likely local to this world. Whoever commissioned this elevator didn't think the carvings were impressive enough, because they were overlaid with gold. We literally rode in a gold elevator. When the doors to the elevator opened to reveal the new floor, white carpet had been replaced with black carpet that had an elaborate design through it in a red so dark it may as well have been black. The walls were black, with gold embellishment. The hallway served its purpose, this was grandeur I had never before seen.

At the end of the hallway were grand double doors opened by two women in matching armor.

I was led into the room. It was a half-circle, with windows on the half circle looking out over the city. On the far side of the room there was a raised dais with four chairs. Two were larger, grander than the two next to them. Behind the four grandiose chairs stood a statue of a long, serpentine dragon with webbed skin between its claws, and graceful wings that stretched over the chairs. Three of the chairs on the dais were occupied. An old man in a black suit embroidered with dark red, wearing an elegant metal crown inlaid with dark red sea glass, gold, and black gems. To his right sat a young man in a wrinkled shirt, with messy hair partially pulled back. Next to Scruffy sat an elegant woman in a simple black dress, her hair in an elaborate coiffure with tiny braids woven through it.

On either side of the dais, there were beautiful chairs set between elaborately carved pillars. Most of the chairs were filled with elegant people who glared at me with near uniform distrust. The only one who had a different expression was the man who sat in the chair closest to the dais, to the left of the woman with the amazing hair. He studied me with analytical interest, like I was some mysterious text he was attempting to translate. When I made eye contact with his extraordinary blue eyes, I felt a brush against my mental wall.

My gaze turned to a glare. Few telepaths were strong enough to even alert me of their attempts to read my mind, few still were strong enough to do it with a cursory search. Whoever this man was, he was at least as powerful as I was, and I had never met an equal so young. He was mid-twenties, so only a few years older than me, with honey blonde hair that was slicked back and a scar across his nose, and another on his lip that curled onto his chin.

I needed to stop staring at his face. It was not the time to be admiring the man, no matter how attractive he was, or no matter that he might be strong enough for me to not need to worry about accidently altering his emotions to my benefit.

I turned my attention forcefully to the interrogator, who bowed to the old man, in unison with the other guards. I didn't know if I was expected to bow, but I awkwardly followed their movements, then stood up straight and held my head high, careful not to let my gaze wander to the attractive man.

"Your majesty," my interrogator said.

"This is the Nexan requesting asylum?" the old man asked. "She's younger than I thought."

"Her forged paperwork says she's twenty-three. Our medical scan shows she's twenty, perhaps twenty-one," my interrogator said. "Our medical scan also showed something interesting about her DNA," he bowed again and held out the screen.

A thin man walked from behind a pillar and took the screen from my interrogator. He took the screen to the old man. The old man read the screen, then glared at me.

I rolled my shoulders back and glared back. I didn't know exactly what they found in my DNA, but I would face the fallout with whatever pride I had left.

The old man handed the screen to the rumpled man next to him. He read the screen and shook his head. "There is a reason we cut contact with Talaraine." He stood and walked off the dais to the attractive telepath. He handed the screen to him. "What do you think?"

The man read the screen. Seriously what was so important?

"Your name is Hope, isn't it?" the man asked.

There was nothing to be gained from trying to continue the lie, but how did he learn my name?

"You have me at a disadvantage, I don't know anyone here," I said sarcastically.

He smirked. I tried not to react. Good grief, it was absurd how much this man affected me.

"My apologies. I am Lord Rowan of the Noble House of Argentia," he stood up and gestured to the rumpled man next to him. "This is Crown Prince Remington of the Royal House of D'Valoria, his uncle, King Vincent of the Royal House of D'Valoria, and Prince Remington's wife, Crown Princess Estelle of the Royal House of D'Valoria."

I glanced at the others in the room, but no one expected an introduction. Which was excellent because there was no way I could remember all those names. I did wish my interrogator had bothered to offer his name.

"What House are you from, Hope?" Lord Rowan asked.

I shook my head. "I ran away from Nexa, I have no House," I said honestly.

"No House on Talaraine?" Lord Rowan asked archly.

I clenched my teeth together and shook my head. "I have no House."

"Are you certain?" he asked.

My DNA. It must connect me to a House's bloodline. I would be lying if I claimed I wasn't curious, but I had made my choice, and my future didn't lie on Talaraine with unknown relatives. I had faced enough rejection in my life.

"I have no House, and I did not ask for asylum on Talaraine. I asked for asylum here."

"You are from an enemy world, you cannot be granted asylum without a sponsor," King Vincent said.

"I'll sponsor her," Lord Rowan said without hesitation.

"Do you understand what that means? She will be your responsibility," the king said.

"Understood, your majesty," Rowan said promptly.

"Do you accept his sponsorship, Miss Hope?" King Vincent asked.

I glanced at Lord Rowan. Why did he make that offer? What was on that screen?

"I...accept," I said slowly.

"Remove her bindings," King Vincent ordered. "Her asylum request will be granted, for as long as she remains her sponsor's charge."

My interrogator removed the shackles and winked.

He and the guards bowed to the king and marched out of the room, leaving me alone with the King and his silent council.

"Your Majesty, who is this girl?" one of the council members asked.

"A Nexian, seeking asylum on Karabeeya," King Vincent said.

"Then we owe her nothing," another council member snapped. "We should ship her back to Nexa and let them deal with her desertion."

"You're advocating death, General Thorn?" Princess Estelle asked archly. "That is the fate of all who attempt to escape Nexa and fail. I've been told it's a slow, torturous, public death, designed to discourage others from making a similar attempt."

"If that bothers you so much, we can drop her off on Talaraine."

"I have spoken," The king snapped. "If Lord Rowan retracts his protection, we will decide where to send her then."

Great, so I was at the mercy of a stranger.

"Take her out of here, and get her cleaned up, she looks like a vagrant," Prince Remington said.

How rude, Scruffy was insulting my appearance.

Lord Rowan stood, bowed to his king, and walked to my side.

"If you'll follow me, Miss Hope?"

I shrugged slightly and walked with Rowan, trying not to gawk and trying harder to ensure I wasn't blushing. Once we were out in the hallway, I risked speaking to him.

"Am I a pawn then?" I asked.

"We are all pawns," he said briskly. "That is the nature of the royal courts, as I'm sure you are already well aware."

I winced; it was much the same on Nexa.

"You have a family on Nexa?" he asked.

"Not anymore. I wouldn't have left if I did."

"Ah, that old expression. Nexa residents do not leave, do not abandon their purpose, to do so is to prove they are disloyal."

"And to be disloyal is to be unworthy of the dirt your corpse rots in, and all who associate with you are to be tested," I finished for him. "It is best to end your own life before committing acts of disloyalty, lest your friends and family are killed for your treason too."

"Did your family escape Nexa?" Rowan asked.

I felt my stomach twist. I shook my head. "Not exactly. I escaped alone." My brother was likely dead long before my father thought of treason, and my sister was clever enough to escape a mining ship. Of the three of us, she had the best chance of finding a happy life.

I crossed my arms as we stepped onto a cold elevator.

Rowan took off his jacket and draped it over my shoulders.

"Thank you," I said. I gripped the jacket and breathed in the scent of his cologne on the fabric.

The elevator went down.

"We're going to the hundred and eighth floor," he said. "That's my floor."

"Hundred and eight, and we're going down? I've never been in a building with a hundred and eight floors."

"There are two hundred floors in this building. it's the grandest building in Veritas."

"What do you do with two hundred floors in a single building?" I asked.

"The lower levels are museums, next offices and meeting rooms. Then the libraries, the employee's quarters, and the nobles' quarters. Then the royal family's quarters, then the grand audience chamber we were just in."

He pulled a small screen out of his pocket and tapped on it. "Your rooms should be ready soon; I'll give you a tour of the rest of the floor while we wait."

"Rooms? Why would I need more than one?" I asked.

"I thought you would appreciate some space separate from me and my daughter, although you are welcome to use the public areas whenever you wish."

"You have a daughter?" I asked as the elevator doors opened, and we stepped into the hallway. Unlike the floor we left, this floor had hardwood instead of carpet, and a blue tinted white paint on the wall.

"Athena, she's nine."

"I guess you're older than I thought, if you have a nine-year-old," I said without thinking.

"I'm likely as old as you think. I had Athena when I was sixteen."

"I didn't mean to pry," I stammered. I couldn't imagine having a kid at sixteen, although my adopted parents took me in at seventeen.

"I offered the information." Rowan said crisply. He opened the door to the right and humidity hit me in the face with a crisp smell of faint chlorine, along with the relaxing sound of water tumbling over rocks. I stepped into the room. It contained a large, deep, pool designed to resemble a pond with a waterfall flowing into it.

"This is beautiful," I said. I touched one of the decorative rocks near the doorway. It was damp.

"You can swim here anytime."

"I can't swim," I admitted. "I've never had the chance to learn."

"Hmm, well, there's the smaller pool, it's not as deep," he moved around three of the larger rocks, and the smaller pool came into view. It wasn't big enough to swim in, but it did look big enough, and deep enough, for several people to sit in and be nearly fully submerged.

"Hope, I mean no disrespect, but please do not attempt to swim without an experienced swimmer, and do not agree to watch Athena in pool without an experienced swimmer, no matter her argument."

"Those rules are easy enough to follow," I said with a shrug.

"Excellent, this way," Rowan said. He walked back into the hallway. And opened the next door on the right. It led to a comfortable room with chairs and four desks, as well as small sitting areas.

"This is my office."

"There's room for twenty people in here, easily," I commented. "Your staff?"

Rowan shook his head. "I do have meetings here, occasionally, but it's usually me and Athena in the evenings. She does her homework here, and I read reports."

I nodded. There was nothing for me to do in this room then.

We moved on, in addition to the office, there was a sitting room, a dining room and a large kitchen. Rowan showed me the doors to his room, and Athena's room, but did not take me in either room.

When that was done, I saw two people get on the elevator at the end of the hallway and Rowan checked his screen.

"Your rooms are ready, I had them add a few things to make your stay more comfortable."

"When did you have time to arrange that?" I asked. "You were giving me a tour."

"I was multitasking." He opened the door across from the room with the pool and we stepped into a room slightly smaller than his office, with a kitchen area in one corner, and a sitting area in the center. On the far side of the room was a door that led into a small bedroom with a huge bed that took up most of the space. There was a bathroom connected to the room. The area was perfect, and far better than any room I ever had.

"Multitasking just means you don't think a specific task is worth your full attention," I teased. I sat in the chair in the corner of my bedroom and looked at Rowan. I almost didn't want the answer to my question, yet not knowing had to be far worse than reality.

"Why am I here? Why did you offer to take me in, give me this room? I doubt that was a popular decision."

"It was a decision only I could make. If I had not made it, you could have ended up being sent back to Nexa. I'm not sure they would have agreed to send you to Talaraine."

"Okay, thank you, but why? What role does this pawn play?"

Rowan sat on the bed. His perfect posture slouched ever so slightly, and he looked down. "I… wanted to prove to the courts of Aquarius and Valoria that not all on Talaraine are bad. I wanted to show that a son of the Eoness could willingly befriend an Aphlia Novem."

I knew I was a Novem, the defendant of nine supposed demigods, but most people viewed us as natural leaders and heroes, not as someone whom befriending shows grand compassion. I had never heard of Aphlia.

"And after you've proven your point, then what becomes of

me?" I demanded.

Rowan shook his head, clearly bewildered.

I wanted to press the issue, but we were interrupted by a young girl opening my bedroom door.

She was certainly her father's daughter. She inherited Rowan's honey hair, although it was wispy on her, and his serious blue eyes. She looked from me to Rowan.

"I thought Rose came to visit. The door to the guest room was open."

"Athena, this is Hope. She'll be staying with us for a while."

Athena glared at me then turned her attention back to her father. "Dad, you never let the women trying to court you stay with us. Why is she different?"

"Athena!" Rowan snapped.

I laughed, recognizing a preemptive attempt to scare me away. "I'm not here to court your father, I promise."

"Then why are you here?" Athena demanded.

"Hope is a refugee, I'm her sponsor," Rowan said.

Athena visibly relaxed and turned to me with a genuine grin.

"Where are you from? Do you know any hand-to-hand combat?"

"Athena," Rowan said.

"No, it's okay. I'm from Several places, and I know some close-range combat. I'm fairly decent with a staff and knives."

"Staff?" Athena asked.

"Well sure, you can find a long stick in a lot of places, so it's a good skill to have when you can't or won't carry a weapon everywhere."

"That's a very practical mindset," Athena grinned. "Will you give me a demonstration?"

I shrugged. "Why not?"

"Perhaps tomorrow, after we take Hope shopping for clothes, if you get your homework done tonight," Rowan stipulated.

"Fine," Athena said. "Will you help me? I don't understand

my math, and Dad's not particularly good at it either."

Rowan bit his lip to hide a self-deprecating smile.

"Well, I might do it differently, but we can look at it," I offered.

I helped her with her homework with some limited success, then ate the dinner Rowan prepared while I helped Athena.

Crawling into that bed was a truly unforgettable experience. The bed was designed different than the bed I had on Nexa and was nothing at all like the stiff pallet I had on the refugee ship. This bed perfectly contoured to me as I spread out, giving the perfect sensation of weightlessness and comfort. I pulled the blanket up around my chin and for the first time in a long time, I fell quickly and deeply to sleep.

# Chapter Two

That was my first mistake.

Normally I laid in bed for a while, building up my mental wall and shielding myself from outside attacks, but I felt safe, and it was the first night I ever spent alone, with no worries at all.

My dream was of a glass room, with a translucent glass floor, and furniture sculpted from glass, more art than function.

I looked around in wonder. It was truly a beautiful room.

"Young goddess, Impertinent whore."

I looked around. There was no one else in the glass building, but I knew the voice, and only one person called me a goddess, my insane grandmother. I was fortunate only in knowing that she wasn't a biological relation, but she was the focus of every misery and pain I experienced in my life. She was convinced that with the right motivation, usually enough suffering, I would somehow gain the power of a goddess. It was her driving obsession, but no matter what she did, I somehow managed to fall short of whatever she wanted to see.

"What do you want?" I whispered.

"What do *I* want?"

I turned, a beautiful woman stood before me, with a cruel smile and long, wild black hair that fell to her knees.

"What do you want?" I repeated.

"You disappoint me, the Goddess of War should never run

from her duty. You swore an oath to aid the leaders of the House of Deva."

"I never swore that oath," I hissed.

"Hmm, your predecessor did. You are bound by it."

"And you're insane, I'm no goddess."

She sighed and looked into the distance with frustration and sadness. "Then I'll have to try with another generation. Again!" she turned back to me and bit her lip.

I felt crushing sadness, pain, but not physical.

"You know the penalty for fleeing? I will find you, and I will kill those who aided you."

I could see it, Athena's mangled body gripped in Rowan's bleeding arms. I could see them all laid out in a neat row, Rowan, Athena, the king, the prince and princess, and everyone else in that room, all marred by the injuries sustained by torture. This was the only future that awaited me, to watch them die one by one before eventually dying myself once I was too broken to beg for death.

"There is one way to avoid this fate, now that you have proven yourself a traitor."

Of course, there was only one way. No one else would suffer for me.

I jerked awake and rolled out of the bed, standing to ensure I didn't fall asleep again. My heart raced, and I was too keyed up for someone who had just woken from a nightmare. I tugged on the oversized t-shirt I wore over shorts and quietly slipped out of my room and across the hallway.

There were dim lights on around the pool, casting the water in an eerie light and shadow dance. I sat down next to the waterfall and let my feet slip into the cool water.

The image of my new acquaintances lined up and dead pressed on my mind. Megaera was insane, worshipped as a goddess on Nexa, and sometimes I wondered if she believed it herself, but I knew she was capable of fulfilling her threat. I had seen firsthand what happened to those who fled Nexa and were later captured.

There was only one way to stop her killing spree. She never went after the friends and family of those who took their own life.

I fingered the faded, nearly invisible scars on my wrists. Straight and thin, from my palm to the middle of my forearm, and studied the cool water.

I had no idea how to swim, had never seen it done, although I had read accounts. If I slipped into the water, would I simply sink to the bottom? Rowan clearly thought there was some risk to me getting in the water unsupervised. Would drowning be quick?

I shifted, preparing to slip into the water, when I heard a loud splash. Startled, I shifted back onto the ledge and looked around. The pool was calm, the splash didn't come from there.

Footsteps, then Rowan stepped around the decorative boulders. I had forgotten about the smaller pool, and I nearly forgot the dark thoughts that brought me to the pool when I saw Rowan, shirtless, barefoot, and soaked, his damp hair clung to his forehead in a tangled mess. I had never seen anyone look so perfect.

Good grief. This attraction was getting out of hand.

"I thought I was alone, I'm sorry," I said awkwardly.

"The water helps me think," Rowan said. He sat down on the ledge where the pool curved, so he was practically facing me.

"It's peaceful here," I commented, uncomfortable. I hadn't thought of my mental wall, and as I quickly built it back up, I realized a strong enough telepath, like Rowan, could get at least a passing read of my emotions from the time I walked into his range.

"Are you alright?" He asked, confirming my suspicion.

"I'm fine."

"Hope, I know when you're lying."

"Thanks Rowan, but you aren't that powerful," I said sarcastically.

He shook his head. "You have a tell. It's subtle, but consistent."

"What is it?" I asked. I considered myself an excellent liar, to be told otherwise was an insult to my existence.

He laughed. It was soft, and when he stopped, I made it my

personal goal to someday make him laugh again.

"I would lose my advantage if I revealed that," he said.

"You have every advantage here," I said, with more bitterness than I intended.

"I'm sorry, I really am grateful for everything you've done, I am. I don't mean to suggest otherwise," I said quickly. I ran my fingers through the cool water and gently kicked my feet.

"I can't imagine what it would be like, to be at the mercy of a stranger's actions." His gaze lingered on my hair, and the white streaks that declared to the universe that once upon a time, my mind was not my own, and I was a puppet for another's amusement.

"I don't need pity," I said. I slapped my hand in the water.

"What happened?" Rowan asked. "No pity, maybe I can help."

Maybe he could help. He was a telepath, and he was strong.

"Are you familiar with the Dream Realm?" I asked.

Rowan nodded. "Here it is referred to as the Betwixt. It's a dangerous place, many have been trapped there only to die here. Why would you go there?"

"I didn't mean to. I normally make sure my mental wall is firm before I fall asleep, but I didn't, and Megaera found me."

"Who is she?" Rowan asked.

I shrugged. "She's Prince Setne's consort, and the people of Nexa worship her as a goddess. She's furious I ran away."

"And if she was in the Betwixt, she's a telepath, is she the one who..." he looked at my hair again.

"Every time she successfully took control of my mind, a lock of hair turned white," I said. I fingered my hair. "I dyed it at her command, I guess I should go back to dyeing it."

He shook his head. "It shows what you survived, I don't think you need to hide that, although if you truly want it, I can arrange for someone to color your hair for you."

I shook my head. "It's a never-ending nightmare to dye it, my hair grows so fast, besides, I haven't had any new white streaks in a couple of years. I can kick her out of my head, but she can still manipulate my emotions."

"Pushing depression to suicide?" he asked.

I looked at the water. "A temporary lapse. I would have shaken out of it before I jumped in the water." Probably.

"Would you object to an exam from a healer?" he asked, uncomfortably.

I snickered. "It's fine, I'll figure out how to block her from manipulating my emotions. I figured out to stop her from controlling me completely."

Rowan nodded, then slipped into the pool.

"Then may I offer you another suggestion?" he asked. His head bobbed gently in the water, and I could see his feet didn't come close to touching the bottom of the pool.

"Sure?" I didn't have to follow the suggestion at any rate.

"Come into the water, I'll teach you a couple of simple basics, so if you ever do slip in, you won't immediately drown."

I shook my head. "I'd sink to bottom."

"No, lesson one, I will never let you drown. As long as you are with me, you are safe in the water." He held his hand up to me.

"So, what exactly do I do?" I asked. "Just jump in?"

"Slide in, keep your hand on the side and if you go under the water just hold your breath and wait for me to pull you back up. Whatever you do, no matter how panicked or tempted you are, do not breathe in the water, or you will see a healer."

I slid into the water. My shirt immediately bellowed around me as I clutched the side of the pool.

"Here," Rowan pushed my shirt under the water, as soon as it was heavy enough, it stopped trying to billow as much, then he moved so he was next to me on the ledge.

"Lesson one, kicking your legs. Stretch them out and kick from the hip, not the knee," he demonstrated with his own legs showing them gliding effortlessly through the water.

I mimicked the movements and laughed as it pushed me against the ledge.

"Using your legs to push the water will help you get back to the surface if you fall in, the second lesson is easier. Give me your hands."

I stared at him wide eyed. "You can't think a thirty second lesson is enough to get me in the middle of the pool?" I demanded.

"I have you, I promise."

I moved on hand to his, then the other. True to his promise, I stayed above the water, although my kicking wasn't nearly as efficient as his. He kept me close, and somehow kept us both above the water.

"Now, close your eyes and lay back."

"Into the water?"

"No Hope, under the waterfall. What do you think we are doing? You'll be fine."

I smirked at the unexpected sarcasm and did as he asked. He held my back and my hand.

"Relax your legs and arch your back," he whispered.

I did as he commanded, surprised he was strong enough to hold me up with one hand in the water.

"Now, stay exactly like that, and don't panic, I'm going to let go, but I'll stay close."

"I'm trusting you," I joked.

I felt Rowan's hand slowly leave my back and I resisted the urge to lash out and grab him. Once the second of instinctual panic was over, I realized I was floating in the water.

"I'm not sinking!" I said with a laugh.

"No, you are doing great, you're a fast learner," Rowan encouraged. He took my hands and I moved out of the floating position and back to facing him, my feet treading the water as he helped keep my afloat.

I looked into his eyes. He was so close, and the intensity and excitement in his eyes startled me. I looked down at his chest, were a faint scar curled from his heart to his shoulder. That scar was safer than looking into his eyes and revealing my own pathetic attraction to this kind man.

"I think that's enough for lesson one," he said finally. He pulled me to the ledge and helped me climb out of the pool before he climbed out on his own.

"I should probably get cleaned up," I stammered, still unable to look at his eyes. "Do you have any scissors? Maybe the white in my hair won't be so obvious if I cut the black out."

"Do you want me to cut it for you?" Rowan offered.

I fingered the ends at the back of my neck and shook my head from one side to the other.

"You could probably do a better job," I admitted. "Meet me in my sitting room in an hour?"

My sitting room was already occupied when I walked back to my rooms. Athena sat in one of the chairs, reading from her screen.

"Good morning," I said haltingly.

"I came to give you this," she pointed to the bag at her feet. "I thought you'd prefer it to your old clothes or dad's shirt." She smirked and made a point to look at the puddle that was quickly forming under my feet.

"Do you have an aversion to towels, Miss Hope?"

"I wasn't planning on a swimming lesson this morning."

Athena raised her eyebrows and shook her head. "Clearly." She handed me the bag, inside there was a silky black wrap dress, stretchy slippers, and a stretchy top and shorts.

"Thank you, where did you get this?"

Athena shrugged. "Dad gave me two trunks filled with my mother's favorite dresses and all of her jewelry. I think you're taller than she was, but the dress should fit close enough."

"Athena, what happened to your mother?" I asked nervously.

Athena rubbed her nose and shrugged. "She and Dad lived on Talaraine for a while, but there, people don't think Novem, and Dragons should have kids, so when I was a baby, this group came into our house and killed her." She held up her shirt, exposing a long scar from her navel to her chest. "They tried to kill me too, but Dad stopped them. He has scars from it too."

Then what exactly was he trying to prove by protecting me?

"I'm sorry," I wasn't sure how to articulate my regret. Was I sorry for asking? I knew it was likely a painful subject so claiming otherwise would be an insult to her intelligence and mine. I was sorry it was such a violent loss, and I was sorry there was such narrow-minded hatred in the universe.

Athena shrugged. "I don't remember her. You can't miss what you never had. Besides, I have a great dad. That's enough." She stood and stepped to the door. "You're going to get sick if you keep dripping like that. I should let you get changed." She slipped out of the room.

A quick shower in hot water and several towels later, I was clean, dry and in the slightly too small clothes Athena left me. I wasn't just taller than Athena's mother, I was curvier. Rowan stood in the center of my sitting room, next to a stool he pulled from the kitchen area.

"You really trusting my dad to cut your hair?" Athena called from the kitchen.

I shrugged. "I'm impatient, I don't want to wait for some hair person to have time to cut it."

"Do you care if she watches?" Rowan asked.

I grinned at Athena as I sat on the stool. "She might learn something."

"Like what?" Athena demanded.

"If he does a decent job, you'll learn something about how to cut hair. If he does a terrible job, you'll learn not to let him cut your hair," I joked. Neither of them laughed or even cracked a smile. Instead, Rowan gently began to comb through my still damp hair. Once he was satisfied that there were truly no tangles in my hair, he slowly lifted my hair, one tiny lock at a time, and snipped it.

The process took longer than I anticipated, but I didn't object, move, or try to focus on the sensation of his fingers running through my hair.

"It's passible," he relented when he finished.

I felt the shorted tips of my hair. It fell around my chin, although there were shorter layers, nearly to my ears. Somehow, all of my hair felt softer with the absence of the dead inches of over-dyed hair.

"That's a lot better," Athena commented.

"Go look in a mirror," Rowan said quietly.

I hopped off the stool and walked into the bathroom, where a mirror hung on the door. My hair was beautiful, and the white streaks weren't quite as noticeable without the damaged black tips.

When I stepped back into the sitting room, Athena was alone.

"My dad said to keep you company while he talks to Remy. It might be a while, Remy is dumb."

"Who is Remy?" I asked.

"Crown Prince Remington."

"Prince Remington is your future leader," I said, although I failed to suppress my smirk as I spoke.

"Kings don't have to be smart; they only have to be willing to listen to smart people," Athena recited.

"Your father said that?" I asked.

"Of course not. Dad only insults people to their face. Aunt Rose said it."

"And your Aunt Rose doesn't only insult people to their face?"

"Aunt Rose never insults people to their face."

That was truly valuable information, to know that Rowan would let you know exactly where you stood with him, and while Rose wouldn't, she would willingly share her opinion with others.

"Does your Aunt Rose live in the building?"

Athena shook her head. "The peace treaty calls for one land dragon from D'Valoria line to live in the Eoness's palace, and a member of the Asea line lives with the Royal family of Valoria."

"I thought your house name was Argentia?" I asked. "Not Asea?"

"Argentia is a Noble House that died out. The king gifted the name, and the lands that came with it, to my father after he saved Remington's life. It gives my father rank and status separate from the status as a lesser prince of Aquarius. It's why so many Families want him to marry their daughters, a noble title in Valoria, and being the Eoness's son makes him the best available option in

Valoria and Aquarius for an advantageous marriage."

I cringed. I thought the women who would attempt to flirt with Rowan were doing to because he was kind, and attractive, and smart, and had that amazing half smile. From the way Athena talked, Rowan could have been a crusty, cankerous, old pervert and these families would have still sent their daughters to court him.

"My apologies," Rowan said, walking back into the room. He handed me a delicately carved wooden box, the size of my palm.

"What is this?" I asked.

"The medallion is programmed to your DNA, and grants you access to different areas in the building. You need to have it on you when you leave this floor, or you won't have access to move through the building."

I opened the box. On a velvet cushion sat an intricate metal disk with a carving of a hard-shell creature with fins and a narrow head. The shell had complex geometric patterns.

"I like it," I said, fingering the design.

"The sea turtle is the family crest of Argentia," Rowan explained. This shows you are here as my guest."

"Thank you," I took the necklace out of the box and slipped it over my head, then, realizing that neither Athena nor Rowan had their pendants visible, I slipped mine under my dress.

"Is the necklace a tracker?"

"Of course, it's a tracker, but you can take it off on this floor, or outside the building."

I shrugged. It wasn't the first time I wore a tracker, and at least I knew about this one from the start.

"Everyone wears them in the building, even the king," Athena said. "Besides, you need it for shopping. You need clothes that fit you, and clothes that are appropriate for wearing in the building. Now come on," she moved out of the room and to the hallway. We followed her. She tapped the wall next to the elevator then held her arms out.

"I summon the elevator!" she jumped back, then frowned. "Wait, let me try again." She tapped the wall again, nodded to herself. "I summon the elevator!"

This time the wall slid open, revealing the elevator.

"Wow!" I said, trying to be encouraging and adequately impressed.

"It would have been a lot cooler if I had done it right the first time," Athena said sullenly.

"I still think it was cool," I encouraged. "I wouldn't have thought to do that."

We stepped on the elevator and rode it down to one of the lowest floors in the building.

The doors opened. This hallway was different. Instead of doors, there were elaborate archways carved with flowers or waterfalls, and inlaid with gold.

"This is where you can get clothes," Athena said.

"We'll start here," Rowan said. He led the way through an archway carved with creatures that were half human, half fish.

"These are interesting," I said, brushing my finger across the carving of a woman with a long fin instead of legs.

"Sea Dragons in their second form," Rowan said.

"I thought dragons were the size of small spacecraft, and not humanoid. Considering how often people talk of them here, I thought I would see one by now."

Athena laughed. Rowan gave her a stern look, that eventually halted the laughter, then faced me.

"Dragons have three forms. You are referring to third form, or true form. Dragons are huge, some have feathers, or scales, or fur, wings or fins or claws or a combination, depending on the type of dragon.

"First form is as humanoid as you or me. You would never know a dragon just by looking at them or talking to them when they are in first form. Second form is the between form, part human, part dragon. It takes considerably less magic to go from first form to second form, than for a dragon to go from first form directly to third."

"Is this an accurate depiction of a dragon's second form?" I asked.

"It's perfectly accurate. Do you see the lines on her neck?" Rowan pointed to the carving. She had thin lines down the sides of her neck on both sides.

"Are they scars?" I asked.

"No. These are gills. Sea Dragons in their second and third forms have both gills and lungs. Lungs allow them to breathe air, gills allow them to breathe underwater. Most depictions don't show the gills, they aren't considered attractive."

"Some even say they're hideous," Athena said sadly.

I fingered the carving again, feeling the faint variation in the gills. "They aren't ugly, just interesting."

"Well, quit looking at the carvings. This shop has the best training gear!" Athena said.

The shop was set up with metal wire mannequins wearing various outfits, but there was no stock I could see.

"Do we take the clothes off the mannequins?" I asked.

"Of course not," Rowan scoffed. He pointed to the small black glass plaques at the base of the mannequins. "You select the outfit piece, and the fit, then you get measured and the packages are delivered to your rooms."

"That simple, huh?" I murmured. I approached one manne-quin. The statue showed a feminine form mid kick, wearing tight, stretchy leggings and a tank top.

"Good choice," Athena encouraged. "That's pretty common for women to train in. These clothes are very mobile, with just enough padding to save you from a few bruises. The displays show black, but you can choose from a list of color options."

With Athena's help, I selected several training outfits, in-cluding two designed to wear in the water so I wouldn't have to wear billowing clothes during my swimming lessons. After the styles and colors were selected, there was the process of getting measured, which really just consisted of standing on a disk as a light flashed twice.

"Now you need casual wear!" Athena announced.

"How many distinct types of clothes do I need?" I de-manded. For years, I had five sets of uniforms, that I wore at all times. On the refugee ship I had three sets of clothes, which was a luxury compared to many on that ship.

"You will need training, casual, formal and court attire, to start," Rowan said.

"Seriously?" I demanded.

"You live here as my personal guest, there is a standard to maintain. You will also need shoes, and jewelry to go with your selections."

When it came to casual attire, I picked what looked comfortable, in colors that looked appealing. I never realized I had a fondness for the combination of pink and black. Rowan chose the formal and court attire, not trusting me or Athena with the decision. Apparently, what one wore when in formal or court attire sent messages to everyone else, and I had to send the right message.

When we were done finding clothes for me, Athena led the way to a balcony. We weren't nearly as close to the ground as I thought, and this was my first glimpse of what the building looked like. It was a three-dimensional v, the base was a thick v shape, and the two sides gradually narrowed to a point at the highest floors. There were several huge outdoor balconies, as the floors gradually shrank. It was like being on a roof of the building, although this building kept going.

"What's out here?" I asked.

"The wishing fountain, every new resident needs to make a wish and drink from the fountain. It's tradition."

I glanced at Rowan. "I don't know that tradition, but people do come to the fountain here, make a wish and drink from the fountain," he whispered.

I shrugged. "So where is this fountain?" I asked.

"This way," Athena led the way to a clearing.

The woman next to me screamed. I glared at her, then seeing her horrified expression, I turned and looked as a body plummeted from the balcony above us, something streaked after it, but when it hit the paving stones the thing curved away and stopped in the air.

It was the princess, with huge gossamer wings spread out from her back.

The man sprawled on the ground was the broken body of General Thorn. I was the closest, and I did not hesitate.

I knelt next to him and held my hands over his head, where blood was pooling on the paving stones. I had a total of four natural abilities, supposedly. I could use three, telepathy, energy infusion, and healing. I had no idea what the fourth ability was, only that my adopted father was insistent I had another ability and would someday figure it out.

For General Thorn, I only needed to heal. I thought about fixing that head injury, and felt my magic flow from my palms, into his skin. I could sense it all, the bone fragments stitching back together as the brain healed and the swelling subsided. Once the skin was whole, I broadened my magic and let the tendrils spread through his body. Bone stitched back together, muscle healed, swelling subsided, and organs healed. Then my magic found something in the blood. I couldn't identify it, my training had some serious gaps, but my magic sought to heal it. I poured magic into fixing the blood.

"Hope?" Rowan hissed.

"I've almost got it," I whispered. My hands trembled as my magic drew on my own strength and energy. I fixed the last ounce of blood, then the marrow in his bones before my magic cut out and I collapsed. There was a high price to draining magic completely, and I was going to regret it. I should have used some of his.

The first thing I was aware of was the worry, shock, curiosity, and fear. Then the whispers came.

Discordant, overlapping, and completely overwhelming. I couldn't pick out individual words if I wanted to, no more than I could tune them out.

"Help her."

I felt a gentle hand brush through my hair, then silence.

In silence, I could fall asleep. I closed my eyes and relaxed against the cool paving stones.

# Chapter Three

I woke in painful stages and looked around the room. There was a dividing panel near the bed that was not there the last time I was in this room. I tried to sit up, failed, and relaxed against the pillow.

"Are you awake?" Rowan's voice came from behind the dividing panels.

"Why are you hiding?" I asked.

"I needed to stay close to you to shield you while you slept," Rowan said.

"That doesn't explain the panel."

"It's creepy and wildly inappropriate to sit in a woman's room and watch her while she sleeps, especially without her knowledge."

"You have my permission to move from behind that panel," I grumbled.

Rowan stepped out from behind the panel and adjusted his grip on his screen.

"You didn't have enough strength for me to place a shield that would hold on its own."

I tried to sit up on my own, but I didn't have enough energy. Well, it wasn't like I had any pride left. "Please help me up."

Rowan pulled me into a sitting position and held out a small water bottle.

"This will wake you up, but it won't restore your magic," he said. "It's a little bitter.

I took a swig. It was very bitter, but I drank the entire thing. In seconds I felt more awake, and stronger.

"You should probably eat something too."

"How long was I out?" I asked.

"A full day, a full night, and most of another day," Rowan said.

I nodded. "And my magic still isn't back. I've never drained myself so completely."

"You saved his life. When you are up to it, he would like to speak with you."

I toyed with the empty bottle. "He wanted to send me back to Nexa, I don't particularly want to talk to him."

"I can tell him you aren't interested in conversation, though he's stubborn and may seek you out."

"I'll take that risk," I stood up and stretched. Whatever was in that water gave me most of my physical energy back.

Rowan read a message on his screen and looked up at me.

"The resident healer would like to see you, she's on her way."

"I'm alright," I said automatically.

"It's standard, you drained your magic completely, and she wants to verify you are healing correctly."

I shrugged. "I've never had a healer check me unless I was seriously injured or ill."

"If you are treated before something serious develops, recovery is faster."

I sat down on the bed next to him. "Who is this healer?"

"A Novem, like you. Her name is Amara D'Valoria. She was adopted by the late Princess Rachel. She's Remington's sister."

"She's a princess?" I asked.

Rowan shook his head. "A lesser princess. She doesn't have a formal title or responsibilities. She heals. It's a common skill among the Novem."

"I'm aware," I joked. I scratched my head and felt how greasy my hair was. "Do I have time to at least brush my hair?"

"She'll be here momentarily. I can have her wait in your sitting room. I'll wait behind the screen panel so you can get ready."

"How close do you need to be?" I asked as I changed. There was no time for a shower, but I would want one eventually, now that I had the luxury of taking showers as often as I wanted.

"The sitting room and directly on the other side of the door was too far, but I don't know how close I need to be."

I nodded. I would wait until my magic returned then.

I heard the door open as I knotted my hair up in a scarf. I tucked the rest of my hair in the scarf and tapped on the panel. "I'm ready."

Rowan followed me into the sitting room.

"If I block my own thoughts, can I speak to you privately?" Amara was beautiful. Her gold hair was streaked with pale blue and pulled back in a loose braid that ended in thick ringlets. She wore capris that were form fitting until they belled at her knees, a long blue shirt with buckled straps over her shoulders, and a loose cardigan with sleeves that pooled around her. She didn't look like a healer, or even a princess, but who else could she be?

"It's not your mind he's shielding me from," I said hesitantly.

"She was overwhelmed by every mind on several floors at least, and her reach kept expanding. Even my mother doesn't have such a large reach with her telepathy," Rowan said.

"I see," Amara said. She turned her focus to me. "Do you object to his presence?"

I shook my head. "He's okay."

"Sit down," Amara gestured to the chair in front of her. I sat, and Rowan sat on a stool a little way away from us.

"What is your medical history? Any chronic issues? Sever illness? Surgeries or replacements?"

I shook my head.

Amara nodded and held her hands out. I shivered as I felt her magic tendril over my skin, through my muscles, and settle on my bones, lingering over past injuries.

"Hold out your arms," Amara said gently.

I did as she commanded, and she pulled my sleeves away from my wrists, exposing the long scars from my palms to the center of my forearms.

"How did you get these?" she asked with a gentleness that burned.

I shook my head.

"I wouldn't ask if it wasn't important," Amara pressed.

"It was a long time ago; I was sixteen and stupid."

"And what happened?"

"I cut them, and put them under running water," I admitted.

"What treatment did you get?" Amara asked.

"Um, my aunt healed the skin quick, so it scarred," I said with a shrug. "That was it."

"I meant, what treatment did you get for your depression?" Amara whispered with a glance at Rowan, who was trying to ignore us, although I didn't doubt he could hear every word.

"I thought you were here to check on me after my magic drained?"

"You're fine. It was fortunate Rowan was so close and was able to create a telepathic shield before permanent harm was done to your mind," Amara said. "But what you did was reckless and shows a pattern of self-harm with these scars."

"I wasn't trying to kill myself, I was focused on General Thorn," I said.

"But you didn't stop, and considering the way he was healed, immediate injuries first, shows you had the training to know when your magic was dangerously low and to stop healing when it reached that point. You also knew that as a telepath, losing control meant the possibility of losing your mind."

"I didn't think of any of that," I objected.

"So, it's a coincidence that you had an untreated suicide attempt four years ago, and a reckless disregard for your own well-being yesterday?"

I considered lying, puffing up with offence and demanding that she mind her own business, but Rowan was listening, and he knew I had considered jumping into his pool a couple of days ago. Another example that he would bring up if I didn't give her the information.

I exhaled. "Look, my grandmother wants me dead, sometimes she messes with my emotions through the Betwixt to try to get me to end my own life."

"Where is she?" Amara asked.

"Nexa, probably."

Amara nodded. She put her hands over the scars I usually tried to hide. I felt her magic twist over my arms. In seconds, the scars had faded to flawless skin.

"You can heal scars?" I asked with a laugh.

"Yes, it's a matter of understanding where the normal skin twists into scar tissue and correcting it."

"Thank you," I said, admiring the skin.

"I will have a package sent to your room. Can you write?"

I glared at her, that was unnecessarily condescending. "My education doesn't match yours, Princess, but that doesn't mean I didn't get one."

"Not all planets teach writing, replacing it entirely with typing," Rowan said.

"My apologies, it was not my intent to offend," Amara said. "I'm recommending you write out your thoughts, and emotions, and you have a mild chemical imbalance that is adversely affecting her emotions. I will be sending a tonic that will correct the imbalance. Take it once every thirty days and you and I will meet in three months' time to evaluate its effectiveness."

I nodded. "So, am I sick?" I asked.

"It's treatable. It's a treatment you should have received when you were a teenager."

"So, I won't be depressed after taking this?" I asked.

"It's not that simple. That's why I'm recommending the journal, at least until you can develop a sufficient support system here. I am available when you need me. Also..." she hesitated and tilted her head.

"What?" I asked. She reached into her back and held out a

rose-tinted glass. She held it up to me, then to Rowan, who glared at her. He shook his head, a subtle motion that I did not miss, and she put her glass back in her purse with a sigh.

"What is it?" I asked.

"It's your blood, so much love is woven through your heritage."

"What?"

"I see it. A young soldier fell in love with a proud queen. A hapless prince warmed the heart of an assassin. A young man sacrificed all he had, and his love sacrificed more in return. That is your legacy."

"I have no idea what you are talking about," I said flatly.

"There is power in the offspring of soulmates, a power this world has for too long tried to suppress. I wonder what the future holds for your children," Amara whispered.

"What are you talking about?" I repeated.

"I have a gift, for you," Amara said. "From my mother, Princess Rachel."

"I thought…" I stopped myself from talking. I had already had one awkward conversation with a daughter about her mother's death.

"Princess Rachel died ten years ago. Before she died, she entrusted this book to my care, to give to you when you came to Karabeeya. The book was in her care for fifteen years, waiting for this moment." Amara took a book out of her bag and handed it to me. Then, she took a bracelet out and handed it to me. The bracelet had several charms on it, one of which was a small crystal key that looked like it would match the lock on the cover of the book.

"What is this?" I asked.

"It's for you, it was left here twenty-five years ago."

"I didn't exist twenty-five years ago, and no one knew ahead of time that I was coming to Karabeeya, so it couldn't have been left for me."

"It was written by an oracle," Amara said. "Oracles have the power to see the future, or glimpses of it anyway. You are extraordinary." Amara stood and gave a slight curtsy to Rowan. "I will take my leave; you have much to discuss."

She walked out of the room, seconds later I heard the elevator doors open.

"She's weird," I said.

"She's an enchantress, the Enchantress of Love. She rambles on occasion."

I held up the book. "She thinks this was left for me five years before I was born?"

"I suggest you read it. Perhaps it will become clear if it was meant for you or not."

I shook my head and jammed the key into the lock on the cover. It clicked with a slight struggle, and I pulled the strap away from the cover. I opened the book and flipped through it. The first half of the book was filled with written passages, and crappy sketches.  he second half was blank. I turned to the first page and began to read.

Hello my daughter.

I know you are my child, although I am not yet certain if you are a child of my blood, meaning you are the offspring of me and my soulmate, or if I raise you. Sometimes I believe it one way, and sometimes I can't see myself ever being loved with that bond shared between soulmates.

I see you are strong, but you must learn to trust. You must learn to rely on others and lead them. I see you standing strong against an enchanter, surrounded by those loyal to you. I see what you are, a budding enchantress. You think you are born of War, but that is not so.

I stopped and looked up at Rowan.

"This sentence. She's referring to Megaera's delusions, I think," I said hesitantly.

"What delusions?" Rowan asked.

"Megaera is worshipped as a goddess on Nexa. The goddess of life and birth." I sneered. "She has a fixation with death. She loves to watch her loyal sycophants as they torture people slowly, until finally those victims die. She claims I'm a goddess too, the goddess of war, but I didn't ever meet her expectations. She claims if I die, another will inherit the power and she'll train them."

"Why didn't she kill you when she made that decision?" Rowan asked with a frown.

I shook my head. "I've never seen her physically kill anyone. She can manipulate emotion, and she can convince others to kill for her, but I don't know that she is willing to kill anyone herself, and those she sent after me failed. They'll kill anyone who helped me."

"They'll have to reach this system first, and get through the security to reach this planet, to say nothing of getting into the city, or this building. And, as you said, you've defeated them before, and this time you aren't alone."

I looked at the book again. Megaera was delusional, I was not the goddess of war. Still, it was nice to have this oracle confirm it. I flipped through the book, then realized I missed the most important passage of all, a note scrawled on the inside of the cover of the book.

*Written by Millenia of the Noble House of Aphelion for my daughter, I think.*

"My mother wrote this," I said. I ran a finger over her name.

"Did you know your mother could see the future?" Rowan asked.

I wanted to shake my head, but I froze. It explained so much. Mom always seemed to be ready for anything. She'd randomly bring extra bandages to our apartment, and the next day my sister or I would need them. Trivial things like that, usually, but there were other instances. I looked at the skin where my scars were. She saved my life, and I had been so careful to ensure no one could find me that day.

"I didn't know anyone could see the future," I said.

"It's rare, one oracle on either Karabeeya or Talaraine, never more than one in this solar system, and never born on the moon colonies. She's either a dragon or a Novem."

I opened the book again, to a random page.

*I see ice and wind. A union destructive to all who oppose them.*

I flipped through a few more pages.

The accord will take the place of the jealous one.

"Most of this is just random sentences and a few really bad drawings," I said. I opened the book to a rough sketch of a lopsided eye, and showed it to Rowan.

"I don't know what that is," Rowan confessed.

"Yeah," I flipped through it again. "'I see wings and scars and the soulmate trapped in darkness.' What does that even mean?"

"As I said, they see glimpses. I don't think they understand all of the glimpses. She wrote what she understood of what she saw."

"Her handwriting improves as she goes, look at this," I showed him the book again, flipping through it.

"She wrote this when she was a child, I recognize the progression," Rowan said. "Twenty-Five years ago, your mother was how old?"

"Uh, she adopted me when she was seventeen, so twelve?"

"How often did she get these premonitions?"

"I have no idea," I said flatly. "I didn't even realize this was how she was getting her information. It makes sense, but I didn't know before."

"This could represent years then," Rowan flipped through the book again. "This passage makes sense, 'To free a dragon from the cursed enslavement, simply replace the command with one ordering freedom. Best to lower your guard before this is attempted, trust is an important part of this cure.'"

"There are cursed dragons?" I asked.

"On Talaraine, all dragons are cursed."

"I'm not on Talaraine," I said, taking the book back. "I have no plans to go to Talaraine."

"Did you plan on being here?" Rowan asked.

I shook my head. "I think I want to eat something." I set the book and the bracelet on the table. "I'm starving."

"You haven't eaten in two days," Rowan said. "Athena made sandwiches earlier, they are in your fridge, stay there," he stood up and walked to the small kitchen area.

I was more interested in the book than I cared to admit, so while Rowan gathered the food and drinks, I opened the book again, and this time I read the passages in order until I found one that might apply.

"Rowan, listen to this. 'I saw a dragon attack a princess; her gold hair stained with blood. I saw death in three crystals, and the crown shatter in the waves. You need to trust the dragon or the dome shatters.' Do you think she's talking about the same dragon that attacks this princess? And how many princesses are on Karabeeya with golden hair?"

Rowan set the food on the table next to me. "My sisters Calista and Rose are blondes. Poltron's heir is male, and the royal family is small, but no blondes that I know of. The city-states don't technically have princesses. Some have lords, most are democracies. We don't know if that passage was referring to a Karabeeyan princess, or another princess from another world, or someone who looked like a princess, or someone who got the title in a commercial promotion, or someone who hasn't been born yet."

"Maybe it's Prince Remy's future child," I joked.

Rowan nodded. "Well, Elle isn't pregnant yet. Its customary for a new noble couple to go on a retreat for at least two months, no longer than six months. If they return after six months, they tried and failed to initiate a pregnancy. If they return sooner, it's because of pregnancy. Elle and Remy were gone a full six months."

"That's an obnoxious violation of privacy," I murmured.

"That is our way on Karabeeya. The continuation of bloodlines is important to the political stability of the countries here. People want to know if the marital alliance will result in a child."

"But you said these are arranged marriages. How well did the prince and princess know each other before they married?"

"The marriage was arranged a few years ago when they were teenagers. They met then and were amicable to a union. Its technically illegal for a marriage to happen if both parties aren't willing. They did not meet again until the wedding. After they signed the papers, they left for their retreat and have only recently returned."

I tilted my head from side to side as I scarfed down my sandwich and considered his explanation. I supposed people slept with strangers all the time, across the galaxy, yet this felt different, more restrictive than a one-night stand.

"Can I ask about you and your wife? How well did you know her before you married?"

Rowan slowly chewed the food in his mouth before he continued. "We met at the signing ceremony and left for our retreat immediately after."

"And why is this next marriage different?" I asked. "Why do you get to choose?"

Rowan didn't answer immediately, and I kept eating to hide my discomfort in addition to sating my hunger. I shouldn't have pried.

"I am the Head of the House of Argentia, in addition I requested that I chose my own bride, for Athena's sake. It's difficult for other noble Houses to hold rival children in high regard. I didn't want to rely on luck when it came to her stepmother. The King and my mother agreed, although Mother assumed I had someone in mind when I made the request."

His tone made me smile. I knew something of overbearing parents.

"Athena told me how she died, I'm sorry."

Rowan shrugged. "She was a good friend, and a good mother. I cared for her deeply, and she did not deserve death, particularly that death." Rowan was distracted by his screen. "Princess Estelle would like to meet you for lunch tomorrow."

"Why?" I asked with my mouth full. Mortified I covered my mouth and quickly swallowed my food.

"Curiosity, I expect. You healed General Thorn in less than five minutes, and you are new here."

"What can you tell me about her?" I asked. I took a sip of the drink, it was fruity, and the clear liquid gave no hint as to what kind of juice it was, although I probably wouldn't have known regardless.

"I don't know her very well. She seems kind and is interested in being involved in the politics of Valoria," Rowan said.

I finished my juice and stood. After eating, a faint glimmer of my magic had returned, scarcely enough for my own mental wall, but I wasn't planning on doing anything else.

"I'm going to go back to bed. You should get some sleep too."

"I should stay with you, the wall you are building is insufficient."

"You've been up for two days taking care of me. I'm fine, but you won't be if you keep going."

Rowan hesitated. "You'll ensure your wall is secure before you fall asleep?"

"I make mistakes, Rowan, I don't repeat them," I gave him the cockiest grin I could manage, then took his dishes and tossed them and mine in the dishwasher, a small box on the counter that cleaned the dishes in seconds. I took them out of the box and put them away.

"Good night, Hope," Rowan said.

"Get some actual sleep, whatever you are so fixated on, on that screen, can wait until morning," I called as he walked into the hallway.

Once he was gone, I went back to bed and curled up under the thick, amazing blanket. I was careful, as promised, and once my wall was as good as it was going to get, I fell asleep.

And woke far too soon to an obnoxious chirping.

I scratched my nose and searched for the sound, while trying my best not to get too far off the mattress.

I found the source in a screen on the table next to the mattress. I picked it up, when the transparent glass faced me, I could see the message inscribed on it, as though it was etched into the glass with neon green paint.

**Appointment in two hours with Princess Estelle on the balcony of the 190th floor.**

I sat up, the motion enough to convince the screen that I was awake, and therefore it no longer needed to chirp at me. I touched the screen, as I had seen Rowan do with his, and the message was replaced with several icons and thick runes. I tapped each one, finding one that made voice calls, one that gave me access to search a database, one that gave me a list of articles, and one that had messages, the one that woke me, and another from Rowan.

**I hope you find this screen satisfactory. It should have occurred to me sooner to give you your own. Athena assured me this was the best model for you.**

I flipped the screen around. I didn't know anything about these communication devices, so maybe Athena chose a simple one. Determined to get a lesson on all the screens would do at a later time, I climbed out of the bed and freed my hair from the scarf I had left it in.

A quick shower, then the paralyzing realization that I had no idea how I was supposed to dress to eat with royalty. I ruled out the athletic and casual wear and chose the simplest of the dresses Rowan had chosen for me. It was fitted around my torso, and flared out from my hips to my knees, with sleeves that were made of several overlapping straps. The print on the fabric was hard to see, green on green. Since I didn't know what jewelry to wear, I didn't wear any, and applied just enough makeup to make it clear I was wearing some, and that it flattered my green eyes.

Once I deemed myself dressy enough, and hoped I wasn't completely wrong about what I should wear, I slipped on the shoes.

While Rowan's selection included everything from slippers to boots, he didn't seem to have much faith in my ability to walk in heels, nearly every pair was flat, except two. The first was a heeled beauty encrusted with black gems that caught the light in a gorgeous sparkle, the second set was a simple pair of satin pink heels. I did love pink.

I slipped them on and waltzed out of my rooms and into the empty hallway. I hoped the clipping noise of my confident strut echoed through the hallway loud enough for Rowan to realize I could be just a little feminine, when needed.

Unfortunately, when the elevator doors closed, I realized two things, there was likely no one else on Rowan's floor, and I had no idea how to operate the elevator.

After it stayed on Rowan's floor for an eternity, my new screen pinged loudly. I held it up and saw a simple message.

**Which floor is your destination?**

I typed in 190 and the elevator quickly rose.

While I waited, I tried to fix my hair in the reflection off one of the carvings. It was a waste of time. When the door opened, I straightened and walked off the elevator.

A young woman in a shimmering black suit stood directly in my way.

"How can I help you, miss?" she asked congenially.

"I'm supposed to meet Princess Estelle in twenty minutes," I said, checking the time on my screen.

"Your name?" she asked

"Hope," I didn't give a family name. I no longer had one.

"This way, miss Hope," the young woman said, her friendly persona never wavered as she led me onto the balcony and to a cove where Princess Estelle sat, a fair distance from anyone else.

"Oh, I must have had the time wrong," I said uncertainly.

Estelle shook her head and motioned to the chair across from her.

"Please, sit. I was early," she said.

I sat down and gave a quick glance of her clothes. Sky blue pants paired with a flowing white shirt. It was probably as dressy as what I wore, at least I wouldn't look absurd next to her. Her hair was the real beauty. She had silver threads woven from her scalp through the elaborate coiffure of braids and curls.

"So, you wanted to talk to me, Princess Estelle?" I asked, determined to get through this without reflecting poorly on Rowan.

"Please, call me Elle. I wanted to thank you for saving General Thorn."

"What happened, how did he fall?"

Elle bit her lip and glanced around. "There was a concussive blast, although we have not been able to identify the origin. The blast knocked him over the ledge. I tried to catch him, but I wasn't fast enough."

"You had wings?" I said, remembering her hovering above the scene with gossamer wings that looked like they could easily be destroyed.

Elle nodded. "My second form allows for flight, something my new husband and I have in common, although he does not care for flying," there was a wistfulness in her tone. She may have continued speaking, but something over my shoulder caught her attention and she straightened with a just polite enough smile.

"Princess Ellie," a friendly, flirty voice rang out over our table. I turned around and realized I might have been under dressed after all.

The woman who stood behind me was *gorgeous.* Her pant suit was perfectly tailored to her curvy form, and the tiny crystals woven into the embroidery caught the light and strategically drew attention to her most flattering features. When she smiled, a small crystal imbedded in her tooth drew attention to her mouth, I shook my head. There was something hypnotic about those crystals, a strain of magic I didn't immediately notice.

"Lady Gabi," Lexie said with a perfectly polite tone that seemed completely different than her conversation with me, more formal, more distant.

"Do you mind?" Lady Gabi sat in the empty chair to my right and faced me.

"You must be Miss Hope, Rowan's dear childhood friend who has come to help him select a bride, since he's struggling to find one on his own, right?"

"Uh," I glanced uncertainly at Elle.

"It's a secret, I know, but my family is well informed," Lady Gabi continued.

Not well informed enough if she was taking some random rumor as fact.

"This is, indeed, Miss Hope," Elle said. "Hope, this is Lady Gabi, her family owns the largest landlocked holding on Valoria."

Lady Gabi grinned at Elle, then turned her attention back to me.

"I was wondering if you could tell me Lord Rowan's

favorite color and favorite pastimes? I would like to commission a dress for the Equinox celebration and need enough time to ensure it's ready."

I gave her a smile that matched her fake one. Since Elle did not correct her assumption, I wasn't going to. There was something I really didn't trust about this woman. She used magic to draw attention to physical features, and I suspected her favorite features had been enhanced with surgery. I suspected this friendly, flirty persona was another enhancement designed to help her get what she wanted.

I was tempted to ask her if her interest in Rowan had anything to do with his wealth, but instead I chose the less confrontational route. Since I didn't know the answer to either question, I gave her my second favorite color, since she was unlikely to believe he favored a color as bold and striking as pink, and my favorite way to waste a day, if I ever had the opportunity.

"Rowan has a fondness for blue, and he enjoys solitude in the many gardens in the buildings, as well as activities outside in wooded areas."

"Phenomenal, I have just the dress design in mind, thank you so much, Miss Hope." She stood and curtsied to Elle before she walked away, immediately followed by two men.

"That woman is supposed to be my advisor," Elle said contemplatively. "I don't care much for the advice she gives."

"You didn't correct her assumption that I was Rowan's childhood friend."

Elle smiled and toyed with one of her braids. "Nor did you. I would tell Rowan what you did, so he can support your deception. Lady Gabi is accustomed to getting her way and known to make rather dramatic scenes when she does not. She vilified me in the noble circles when I stopped including her in meetings two days after hiring her as my advisor. It's been an inconvenience."

"I'm sorry," I said.

"Ah, that is politics in the Courts of Valoria. I am new here, untested, and untrusted. Something you and I have in common. I suspect her influence will eventually wane. It happens often enough."

Another woman in a shimmering suit came to the table to ask what we would like for lunch. Since I wasn't familiar with the food of the planet, let alone the offerings in this particular establishment, I ordered the same thing Elle ordered. When she left, Elle continued her conversation.

"Another example of shifting opinion occurred within the council after you saved General Thorn's life. Now those who would have you given citizenship here are more adamant, and the opinion that you should be sent to Nexa has been silenced. General Thorn is your biggest supporter."

"I healed some broken bones. Anyone could have done that."

Elle sighed and toyed with her braid again, I suspected it was a nervous habit the princess either wasn't fully aware of or was unable to break.

"You healed a genetic disorder that had significantly shortened his life span, one that was incurable and exceptionally rare. He will now live to old age, barring some other cause of death, and that was not an option previously."

"That's what was wrong with his blood?"

"Yes."

I shrugged. Elle's sister-in-law thought my heroism was a result of a flagrant disregard for self-preservation, but at least some good came out of it. General Thorn had been the loudest voice calling for my deportation.

The food came, a bright mix of fresh fruits and vegetables drizzled in a tart sauce that made an amazing combination.

"If the process isn't too taxing, I was wondering if you would be willing to give a demonstration of your healing methods to a few of the top healers in the city? There has been a great deal of interest since General Thorn's healer realized the genetic disorder was no longer infecting him."

I nodded. As long as I monitored my magic, I should be able to give a successful demonstration. "When will this happen?" I asked.

"I'm not sure, it will have to be scheduled. I will have my secretary contact all interested parties and arrange it. Expect her to reach out to you after to the Equinox celebration. You are coming with us, correct?"

"I haven't heard anything about an Equinox celebration."

"Ah, *men.* Rowan probably didn't think to ask you yet because your social calendar is not yet filled. Well, inform him that you have a friend in me, and your social calendar will fill as a result."

"Thank you?" I asked, unsure of what she meant exactly by 'social calendar'.

Elle laughed. "Your honesty is a refreshing change. I feel I could ask your opinion on anything, and you wouldn't hold back."

"Yeah, I have this wonderful gift, it's called talking without thinking," I said sarcastically.

After the lunch, I went back to Rowan's floor, and realized I could hear Rowan and Athena talking in Rowan's study. I walked into the study. Rowan was reading something on his screen, and Athena sat on the floor with a pile of sticks and cords.

"What's this?" I asked. I sank to the floor next to her.

"I'm making a model of the 57$^{th}$ floor garden. It's an assignment."

"Do you need help?" I asked, looking at the mess of supplies. It looked like she hadn't even started.

"Yeah, can you hold these two sticks?"

I did exactly as she instructed, letting her make every decision so Rowan wouldn't accuse me of helping her cheat. It was mostly quiet, as Rowan reviewed whatever he was reading, and Athena carefully built her model.

"Done, I'll paint in the flowers and plants tomorrow after the glue dries," Athena announced when the last stick was in place. I looked at the tangled mass of glue, sticks, and cords. It looked like a building went through a blender with a misshapen bush and the end result was immortalized with copious amounts of sticky streams of glue.

Athena seemed unaware of how bizarre her creation looked

as she carefully moved it to the corner of the study, then skipped to the door.

"I'm going to practice," Athena announced.

"Be careful and leave enough time to clean up before supper," Rowan said as he signed the screen and tapped to the next document.

After she left, I picked up my shoes and stood to face Rowan.

"Before I forget, if Lady Gabi asks, your favorite color is blue, and you enjoy spending time outside with plants."

"My favorite color is green, and I enjoy spending time in water, swimming, fishing, and the like," Rowan corrected absently. He read his document for another moment, then looked up at me startled. "How did this come up?"

"Well, there's a rumor, that she took as fact, that I'm your childhood friend and I came here to help you find a bride at the request of your mother."

"That sounds plausible enough to be treated as fact. Thanks to you, blue dresses will be the most common clothing choice among single nobles."

"Good, I like blue dresses," I quipped, I moved to the chair next to his and sank into it.

"Before I forget, Remy is taking his yacht out on the sea to witness the summer solstice sunrise. It's essentially one big, obnoxious party. Athena and I will be on that ship. Athena's class is using the opportunity to stargaze, weather permitting, and I'm still helping Remy get up to date on matters after his six-month retreat. Would you accompany us? Athena requested that I ask you."

It was odd, I found myself wishing that it was Rowan who wanted to go to this big party on the yacht with me, as fond as I was of Athena.

"Sure, it'll be interesting," I said casually. "I think Princess Estelle said something about it as well."

Rowan nodded, and the conversation done, he turned his attention back to what he was reading.

# Chapter Four

I thought I would be bored in the four days between the invitation and the party, but the screen Rowan gave me, combined with swimming lessons, and the training room I found a few levels below, kept me busy.

It had been a long time since I trained with my father, but I relearned the motions fast enough.

The morning we were scheduled to get on the yacht, I woke up to the annoying sound of my screen well before sunrise. At Rowan's insistence I had set the alarm for the cursed hour. Apparently, it was tradition to set sail with the sunrise, which meant getting on the ship well before sunrise.

I forced myself out of bed and took far longer than I would ever admit figuring out how to put the dress Rowan gave me for the departure. Somehow, he figured out my quiet fondness for pink, and the daring bright shade of this dress was absolutely perfect. Unfortunately, it also had several sheer layers that kept getting tangled together as I tried to put it on. Once I got the silk layer that clung to my torso and thighs figured out, the rest still had to be untangled. Once I was done, it was almost worth the effort. The sheer layers floated around me, billowing as I walked and forcing me to walk a little slower, so it didn't tangle in my legs. I once again wore the pink satin heels, doing so made me taller than Rowan and eye level with even the tallest of the noble men.

Once my hair was curled and shimmering makeup applied, I realized I looked nothing like the girl I was raised to be, or the refugee I thought I would be when I first arrived on Karabeeya.

When I stepped out in the hall, Rowan and Athena were waiting, although Athena somehow managed to fall asleep while on her feet, leaning against the wall.

"I didn't mean to keep you waiting," I said.

Rowan held out a large tumbler. "We are not late."

I accepted it and looked inside, a thick, creamy drink that was more soup than beverage. Excellent.

"You look stunning," Rowan commented.

I glared at his suit, a long jacket that fell to his knees over black vest embroidered with black thread and a dark blue, nearly black shirt, paired with crisply pressed slacks and shiny black shoes. Athena was dressed equally sharp and equally dark in a straight black skirt, a sleek black blouse with a blue-ribbon bow for a tie, and a black ribbon holding her hair back. Standing next to them, my dress was loud and mildly obnoxious.

"I think I might be overdressed," I said sullenly.

"You look like a Soul of Caverns Deep," Athena said sleepily.

"What's that?" I asked.

"Ghosts of the brides drowned in the Caverns Deep after the dragons on Talaraine were cursed."

I stuck my tongue out at her.

"You aren't overdressed. You are dressed for a leisure trip," Athena said smugly.

"We're going on the same trip!"

"Our goals are different," Athena said. She stood straighter. "You are going for leisure. I am going for business, for my classes, and as a future candidate for the Elite Guard, I must always demonstrate focus and professionalism."

"You're nine," I objected.

"Yes?"

"Shouldn't you be a kid? Playing in the street or whatever kids do?" I wasn't going to admit I actually had no idea what nine-year-old children should be focusing on. By the time I was nine,

I had practically mastered manipulating other people's emotions and my grandfather was using that skill to quell dissent in Nexa's influential leaders.

"Waste of time, I have goals."

I gave Rowan my best disapproving glare. He shifted and moved to the elevator.

"Right, we should get going," he pressed the panel on the wall to summon the elevator and the doors slid open.

As we rode the elevator down, the longest ride I had taken so far since we were going to the underground garage and I had never even gone to the ground level, I drank my breakfast and looked up 'Soul of Caverns Deep'.

Centuries ago, both Talaraine and Karabeeya were ruled by Dragons, then the Novem came with shiploads of their followers. Not liking the watery conditions of Karabeeya, they ignored it, and settled on Talaraine. There was conflict between the Dragons of Talaraine and the new invaders before they eventually settled into an uneasy coexistence. Eventually, the invaders convinced the Dragon Princess to marry one of their leaders, and in the spirit of unity with Karabeeya, convinced the Eoness of the time of the value of marriages between their nobles and the nobility of Karabeeya, and sent four women to marry Dragons here.

Unfortunately, the alliance on Talaraine was a ruse. The Royalty was killed, the magic of Talaraine bound to the invaders with blood and a curse. Every Dragon on Talaraine was cursed, if they took second form, thought became difficult, and they became ruled by emotions. If they took third form, all trace of sentience was gone. They were trapped, forced to live as the invaders did.

The Eoness was furious, and to ensure the same thing did not happen on Karabeeya, the four brides were taken to the deepest caverns, and then the capsule they were in was ruptured. They died, either from the pressure of the water or from drowning.

Athena had been referring to the legend that those women haunt the caverns, seeking revenge on the Dragons who killed them. The sketches I found of the four showed ghoulish women in dresses that floated around them, not unlike my various layers of sheer fabric.

"Is that what my dress is supposed to look like?" I teased.

Rowan glanced at the picture, then looked at my dress and tensed. It was the only confirmation I needed.

"My apologies, which is not at all what I intended when I selected that dress."

I smirked. "Whatever, I'll rock it."

"If a child can make the connection, perhaps the dress is in poor taste."

I thought back to the pain it was to get the dress on. Changing would be an equal pain and we wouldn't get to the yacht in time.

"If you want to help me, get out of the dress, we can go back." As soon as the words were out of my mouth, I tensed, horrified at what I just implied.

Rowan seemed equally uncomfortable. "The dress is fine, we should stop talking about it," he said quickly.

"Yeah, the dress is fine," I agreed. "This conversation is done."

"You two are weird," Athena said as the elevator doors opened.

I stepped off first and moved to give Rowan plenty of room. The garage was spotless, each car polished and well maintained. It was more like a showroom. Some of the vehicles were low to the ground, some were larger, designed to go over dangerous terrain and carry more people.

Rowan led the way to a sleek car with large, wide wheels. The car was dark green with silver embellishments around the windows. Rowan tapped the passenger door and the backseat door. They twisted up in a smooth motion, sticking nearly straight up.

"I guess that makes it so you could park closer to other vehicles if you wanted," I commented.

Rowan gave me an unimpressed smirk. Athena climbed into the back seat and tapped the curved doorframe three times. Her door twisted back down.

Rowan waited while I climbed into the passenger seat. It curved with a perfect contour to lean back, and there was more than enough legroom.

"Get the rest of your dress into the car," Rowan instructed.

As I gathered the errant fabric, I smirked at him. "I thought we weren't talking about the dress anymore."

Rowan smiled, leaned down, and tapped the door frame three times. The door twisted down and sealed against the car.

"I read this system uses hover technology, not ground technology," I commented after he was in the driver's seat.

"Talaraine does. There's too much rain and erratic wind on Karabeeya for hover technology to be reliable. Wheeled vehicles work better."

"Will it rain while we're on the yacht?" I asked, not fond of the idea of water pouring from the sky to soak everyone and everything, slowly filling the yacht until it sank into the ocean.

"Of course," Rowan replied. "It rains several times every day."

"Yay," I muttered under my breath.

Rowan turned on the car and sped out of the garage. The ride was smooth, like gliding over the road. The road curved and angled up, then we were out of the building and on a surface street. There weren't many other vehicles on the road this early, and Rowan quickly swerved around those that were.

I looked out the window. The tallest building was the one we lived in, but every building stretched high above us, all seeming to touch the dome that shielded the city from the weather.

Rowan drove through a tunnel, as we sped through the tunnel, I saw a rough painting in garish colors. I turned to get a better look at it, but we were already too far away.

"What was that?" I asked.

"Graffiti, unauthorized artwork vandalizing the city. As we approach the gates, we'll be driving through an area that has more. The king arranged a contract with a local company to remove the graffiti, but its repainted just as fast in some areas of the cities. The one we just passed is a gang slogan."

"The king allows his cities to be vandalized?" I asked, surprised. Hiring someone to routinely clean it up did nothing to prevent it from happening.

"It's not allowed. The penalty if the graffiti artists are caught is community service."

"The penalty for damaging public areas on Nexa was death." I said.

"The penalty for a lot of crimes on Nexa was death," Rowan retorted.

"Sounds cruel," Athena commented.

I nodded; my attention drawn to a high metal wall. I wasn't sure how far it went, but I suspected it encircled the entire city. Rain splattered against the barrier, creating a waterfall that flowed to the other side of the wall.

Rowan drove to an opening in the wall, past guards who waved idly, not paying real attention to who was leaving. There was a curved cover from the wall that extended far enough to divert the rainwater from pouring on the vehicles in a sheet, then we were free of the city and speeding through the rain. The water wicked away from the windshield and windows before it obstructed our view. I could see two domes in the distance, and one partially obstructed by the dome over Valoria.

"Why are the cities walled, Athena?" I asked.

"During the dry season, the land outside the cities is dry."

I glanced at the overwhelming foliage and the mud underneath.

"Well, drier. During the wet season, this whole area floods. Sometimes it even reaches the tops of the walls, and they have to use special forcefields to reinforce the barriers and keep the cities from flooding," Athena said.

"What happens to all of these plants when the area floods?" I asked.

"Some die, some thrive under water and are dormant during the dry season."

"Why is it called the dry season? Everything looks wet to me."

"I guess they didn't want to call it the flooded season and the less flooded season," Athena reasoned. "The sea dragons named the seasons. The sky dragons call the seasons the warm season and the cold season. I love the cold season. I'll take you to the top of the wall so you can see this whole area flooded. It's beautiful," Athena promised. "That's about four months from now."

I smiled at her but didn't comment. I thought I would spend my entire life on Nexa, but then things changed. I was no longer so confident in where I would be in the future. Would I still be here in four months? Would I still be part of Athena's life?

"Hope?" Rowan said. "Turn around, there's the ocean."

I turned in my seat, so I was facing forward. Rowan pointed to the left.

I had never seen so much water in one place, even knowing that this world was mostly water. The water curled and crashed against the shore, ripping sand off the shore, and taking it into the water. I couldn't imagine riding in a boat on those swells would be a leisurely trip.

"We're going out on that?" I asked. "Those waves look violent."

"The ocean can be violent," Rowan conceded. "We will not be on the open ocean for this trip. We will stay in the bay, where the water is far calmer."

Rowan drove around a large hill, momentarily obstructing the view of the ocean. Then I saw it, what had to be the bay. A thin strip of land extended out into the ocean, and on the other side of it, was calm water gently lapping against the beach. We drove to the harbor, with rows of boats tied to piers. The first that came into view were crowded with small boats taking all available space, then we passed piers with fewer boats, but those boats, then the piers, gradually grew larger, until the furthest piers each only docked one ship. Rowan drove down one pier and parked next to the ramp to a beautiful yacht, far larger than what I was imagining based on my searches for images of yachts. It wasn't the largest ship in the harbor, but I suspected the largest boats were not intended for a small party, but multiple, simultaneous, large ones.

"This is the prince's yacht?" I asked.

"Yes, there will be a total of 103 guests, and over twice that in staff. The yacht will not be at full capacity, of course."

"Of course," I said sarcastically. The yacht looked like it had five levels above the waterline, and I didn't know how many levels below the waterline. On the deck was a large swimming pool at one end, and a docked land jumper on the other end, with enough room between the two for four hundred people to line dance around the cockpit.

Rowan climbed out of the car, leaving his door raised. He walked around the car before I figured out how to open the door and opened it for me, then opened Athena's door. As soon as we were all out of the vehicle, a young man in as sharp uniform climbed into the driver's seat and slowly drove back to the road.

"Lord Rowan," Lady Gabi called from the deck of the yacht.

Rowan completely ignored her as he offered me his arm. I took his arm as I had seen ladies in the building do and took Athena's hand to keep her from trying to balance on the edge of the pier to show off to the guards.

"I'm not a baby," Athena hissed.

"Just because you can swim doesn't mean you should. If you fall, I won't be able to rescue you. I can't swim remember?"

"Dad could," Athena argued, looking longingly at the edge of the ramp.

I looked at Rowan's suit, pointedly examining the heavy material and the long jacket. "Can you swim in that?"

"Of course," Rowan said, "But let's not test it. Athena, you have a class in less than an hour."

"Yeah, a swimming class," Athena grumbled.

"Why is there a swimming pool on a yacht anyway?" I asked. "Couldn't people who wanted to swim do so in the ocean?"

"Only if they were really good swimmers, and the yacht was stationary, so they didn't get left behind," Athena snickered. "Besides, the ocean is cold."

"Well, since you know so much, where we should go to watch this thing leave the pier?" I asked as we stepped onto the deck.

"The bow. That's the front of the yacht. Come on!" She pulled me across the deck. Rowan trailed behind us at a far less urgent pace. I almost missed Gabi's scowl as we hurried past her.

Athena managed to find a spot along the rail to the left of the center. She climbed onto the rail so she could better see the harbor. I stood next to her, mostly out of curiosity, there was minor risk she could tumble over the railing, she wasn't far enough up on the railing for that to be likely.

"Hope grab the railing," Athena instructed.

I put one hand on the railing, to humor her. After I did so, I noticed Rowan step closer to me. I grinned. Even stuck-up Rowan was excited to see this launch.

The boat surged forward, and I lost my balance. Rowan grabbed my shoulders and gently pushed me back to the railing, where I grabbed on with both hands to keep my balance. In a few moments, I adjusted to the new momentum and hesitantly let go of the railing.

"Would you like to try walking?" Rowan asked.

"What did you have in mind?" I asked.

"A tour, and I can show you your room."

"Sounds great," I turned and followed him to the stairwell. I was unsteady, but since I didn't fall again, I judged my journey a moderate success.

The yacht included a large dining area, a small theater, an indoor pool, and the cabins for guests and staff, and Rowan didn't even give me the tour of the entire yacht. The hallways were far narrower, and the space efficiently used, but the yacht had the same luxurious, wealthy feel as the building.

My assigned cabin had two large beds, although I was the only occupant. There was also a couch that could be converted into another bed. This was a room meant for a family, and I had it all to myself.

The small closet was already stuffed with my clothes, and the small bathroom was stocked with my soaps and cosmetics.

I looked at the two beds, then settled on the one furthest

from the door. Not wanting to fight with the layers of my dress, I kept it on, kicked off my shoes, curled up against the pillow, and fell asleep, grateful for the chance to catch-up on the sleep I missed by waking up in the middle of the night to get ready for this trip.

When I woke, my dress wasn't too horribly wrinkled, and it was time to admit I wasn't taking the thing off because I was too lazy. I brushed my hair back into a close enough style and stepped out into the hallway. In my eagerness to take a nap, I neglected to find out where Rowan and Athena were staying.

"Miss Hope!"

I turned in the hallway, not immediately recognizing the excited, feminine voice that called my name.

Gabi stood in the doorway of another cabin, frantically waving at me.

"Hello Lady Gabi," I said hesitantly. Did she already know I wasn't a childhood friend of Rowan's and that the blue dress she wore wouldn't grab Rowan's attention as she had hoped?

"Come into my cabin! I have a gift for Athena, and I want to know what you think of it."

That was probably a more effective way to get Rowan's attention, if Athena liked the gift. Determined to be more helpful this time, so she wouldn't get suspicious, I walked to her cabin and followed her in.

Gabi's room was larger, and had a more open layout than mine, with a single large bed in the center of the room, and a narrow balcony on the opposite wall.

"It's out on the balcony," Gabi prompted.

That seemed like an odd place for a gift. While it wasn't raining right that moment, it had been earlier, and Rowan said it rained several times a day, every day.

I followed her onto the balcony and saw absolutely nothing.

I turned to her, a question on my lips when she grabbed my wrists and something cold and metallic snapped around them. She released my wrists barely before the metal bracelets snapped together, forcing my hands in front of me against my will. I pulled, but whatever magnetic force binding them together was too strong for me to overpower.

Gabi made a small sweeping motion with her hand, and a cold, metal ring linked to a chain snaked out from behind the curtain of her balcony and snapped around my ankle.

"Are you kidding? I snapped.

Another motion and a thick concrete block skidded out of the room, connected to the chain around my ankle.

I focused on the block with the intent of filling it with enough explosive energy to damage the room, but nothing happened.

"Did you think it would be that easy?" Gabi mocked, her voice cold and dripping with hatred. "Even a Novem will eventually drown."

Gabi made a scooping motion and just like that, I was weightless, floating in the air next to the block. Left with no other option and no way to fight whatever she had done to seal my magic, I let out a loud, high-pitched scream and I kept screaming as she waved her hand and forced me to float over the balcony.

I barely had the sense to stop screaming as I slammed into the water. It was like hitting a hillside, then slowly sinking into the freezing water. The block was sinking faster than I was, dragging me down. I kept my gaze desperately to the reflective light above me. I wanted to take a breath, but Rowan's warning echoed in my mind, and I kept my mouth and nose sealed.

Something dark entered the water above me and swam toward me. I couldn't tell exactly what it was, but it seemed to elongate as it twisted through the water.

When the block hit the bottom of the bay, the thing caught up to me. Hands, with webbed skin between the fingers, grasped the sides of my face. A mouth pressed over mine, and hot breath forced its way against my lips.

I took in a deep breath, inhaling the lifesaving air. The person? Creature? Whatever it was, swam quickly to the surface. I held my breath again, but it hurt and the urge to breathe, no matter the consequences, was nearly overwhelming. Just as I nearly lost control, the blur returned. It put its webbed hands on my face and once again pressed its mouth over mine.

We settled into a routine, the creature made multiple trips to the surface, only to return with more lifesaving air. The rapid swimming back and forth must have been exhausting, but the creature never slowed.

After several trips, there was a longer pause before the creature returned. It gave me another breath of air, then slipped a rigid plastic cover over my nose and mouth. The creature waited, expectantly.

Hesitantly, I took a small breath. The air in the device had a chemical taste that was almost nauseating, but it was still far better than the previous method. The creature didn't leave once I started breathing. I was grateful for the company. It tried to lift the concrete block, but it was too heavy. I couldn't tell what the creature was. It was far too long and slender to be human, it reminded me of a long fish, although it had a humanoid head, shoulders, and arms.

It moved my floating, billowing dress out of the way and tried to remove the ring around my ankle, but whatever it tried didn't work. It swam back to face me and gently put a hand on my face, then it swam up to the surface, leaving me completely alone in the water.

# Chapter Five

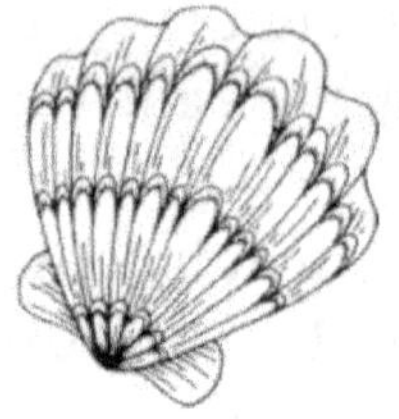

I tried to twist my hands to free them. I suspected the block on my magic was in the shackles on my wrists, and if I could get free, I could use a gentle mix of kinetic energy and pyrokinesis to sever the chain. I wasn't sure if I could swim all the way back to the surface, but at least with the thing on my face I wouldn't drown.

As my arms burned from exhaustion and blood blossomed around my wrists from the friction and pulling too hard, the creature returned with a more humanoid blob. This one was much smaller than the creature, about my height if I had to guess.

The creature moved my dress, so the humanoid had unrestricted access to the chain binding me to the block. It used a small, jagged blade to saw through the links in the chain. As soon as I was free, the creature wrapped me in its arms and sped towards the surface.

As soon as my head broke through the water, I turned to look at the creature clearly for the first time. It looked like Rowan. It was probably Rowan. I knew he was a dragon, but I never thought too much about what that meant. He looked different, with shimmering, pale blue scales on his forehead and splattered over his cheekbones. His eyes were larger, the blue in them darker. There were scales on his arms, and his bare chest. From his torso down was a long, blue, supple, tail, made for swimming in the ocean.

Rowan winced at my awestruck gawking.

"Are you hurt?" he asked. He held me with one arm and tried to check my wrists with his other hand.

I tried to talk, but the thing on my face prevented it. Instead, I shook my head and shrugged.

Rowan took the thing off my face.

"Your wrists."

"I was just trying to get these things off, it's fine. I'm fine," I gasped. I shivered as a cold breeze blew over the water.

"Get in the boat," Rowan pulled me through the water.

I hadn't noticed the boat that floated a short distance away from us.

The humanoid with the jagged blade was climbing a ladder on the back of the boat. He wore a skintight black cover that concealed his head and covered every inch of his body, except his face, which was obscured by a mask.

Rowan pulled me over to the boat and lifted me over the side. The masked man helped pull me over the boat, then immediately wrapped me in a thick towel that didn't exactly provide warmth, but it shielded me well enough from the cold breezes.

I looked around. Prince Remington was sitting at the helm, staring at me with naked curiosity. One of his bodyguards, a stiff man with an impassive face, sat in the seat next to Prince Remington. The man who sawed through my chain took off his mask, which didn't help me identify him, because his back was to me, and he rummaged through a storage box under the benches on the front of the boat.

Rowan climbed the ladder and pulled himself, tail, and all, into the boat. I shifted. The tail was long, and he let it sit over the edge of the boat, but he still needed more room.

He took a slow, deep breath. His tail twitched and spasmed, rocking the boat gently from side to side. His tail shrank and split into two halves. The scales faded from the tail and his skin, his eyes shrank, and in seconds he was just a man. A completely naked man.

I looked away, embarrassed by my temptation to stare.

"That's not the first time I've had to dive into the ocean after your sorry bare ass."

I turned. The man who had severed the chain was none other than General Thorne. He tossed a towel at Rowan, who caught it and quickly covered his lap. Unlike me, he seemed completely unaffected by the cold.

"My apologies," Rowan said breathlessly. He leaned against the side of the boat and closed his eyes.

"Here," Remington moved from the helm to knell in front of me with a small, rectangular box that hummed gently. He held it over my wrists and the humming intensified. The rings restraining my hands fell off and clattered into my lap.

"I've seen these before. May I?" Remington asked.

I let him take the rings. I didn't pay attention to what he did with them, I was distracted by the unexpected surge of my magic. I funneled it into my injured wrists, healing the cuts to flawless skin.

But it wasn't enough to quell the unexpected surge. I felt my head itch, and my mouth *changed* my canine teeth grew longer, sharper.

Shocked by what my magic was doing, I quickly funneled it into my mental wall, strengthening it to the point it would hold for days without further maintenance. My teeth shrank back to normal, and my head stopped itching. I ran my tongue over my teeth. They were back to normal, smooth, dull, and their usual size.

I glanced at Rowan, who stared at me, then shook his head.

"Is everything alright?" I asked uneasily. Remington was too absorbed in studying the rings, leaving Rowan alone to witness whatever changes my appearance went through during that bizarre moment.

"I'm more tired than I realized," Rowan said uneasily. "Are you hurt?" He glanced at my healed hands.

I shook my head and held them up. "I can heal, when I have enough magic, remember?"

My attempt at humor was met with awkward silence. I tried another, more relevant tactic.

"How did you know I was in the water?"

"We heard you scream," Remington said bitterly. "My room is above Lady Gabi's. We were supposed to be at a play, but Elle and Amara found a puzzle and roped me and Rowan into trying to solve it. If that hadn't happened, there would have been a successful assassination attempt on a royal craft."

"Who threw you into the bay?" General Thorne asked. He moved around me and sat down in front of me with a small bag in his hands.

I glanced at Rowan, who somehow managed to fall asleep, still naked, and wet, except for the small towel.

I wasn't sure how to answer his question, so I settled for glancing at Remington, hoping for a clue. What would the price of accusing a noble, one powerful enough to intimidate the crown princess, be? I was Rowan's guest, but in the ultimate hierarchy, I was nothing more than a refugee from a hated world.

"Hope, you have nothing to fear here. I want the truth, no matter what that truth is."

"Lady Gabi," I said reluctantly.

Remington nodded and held up the rings. "That's what I thought." He glared at Rowan's sleeping form. "I told him to be clearer in his rejections, I'm sorry Hope."

"It's not your fault, any more than it's Rowan's," I argued. It wasn't fair for Remington to imply the blame lied with Rowan when Rowan couldn't defend himself.

"When Lydia died, my uncle gave Rowan permission to marry whoever he wanted. It's a tempting offer for nobles to have the chance for a marital alliance merely with Rowan's request."

"You don't think Rowan will fall in love with someone? You really think he's going to marry for some political advantage?"

"Rowan has been entrusted to find an advantageous match on his own. In time, love can come from such a union, and it's encouraged."

I wrapped the towel tighter around my shoulders and

shivered.

"Miss Hope, can I please see your foot? I want to try to unlock the ring," Thorne said.

I moved my foot reluctantly. He had just saved my life, but that just meant we were even, and he could go back to advocating for my deportation.

His movements were efficient, as he selected each tool and worked on picking the lock.

"Why won't the box Prince Remington used on my wrist bindings work on the chain?" I asked as he worked.

"It's more effective to use two distinct kinds of restraints on a victim. With electricity, you can render those rings useless, but it takes a physical key to unlock this one, or hopefully my lock picking kit," he said with a grin. "And…that's it. You are now free. Do you want to keep this?" He held up the ring with the broken chain on it.

"No, toss it in the water," I grumbled.

Remington snatched it from Thorne before he could do as I asked.

"We need that for evidence," Remington said impatiently. "I suspected Lady Gabi was either responsible for throwing you overboard, or involved in the plot, so I had her detained. This will give me enough proof to talk to my uncle."

"What will happen?" I asked.

Remington gave a half shrug. "Don't know, it's been a long time since a noble has been involved in an assassination attempt."

The boat began to move, I turned. Apparently, the bodyguard took over Remington's place at the helm and was piloting the boat back toward the yacht.

"Crowe, when we return, find Rowan some clothes and stay with him. Do not let him make a scene. I'll take Hope back to her room," Remington said.

"I'll go with you," Thorne said quickly.

"I can find my own way," I objected. If getting thrown off the balcony was the result of me being seen flirting with Rowan, I did not want to see what would happen if I was caught walking the halls with the crown prince. If I was being honest, I wasn't comfortable walking with Thorne either. While I had no way to prove it, I suspected the bizarre surge in my magic was somehow connected to him, although I didn't even know why I suspected that.

"And risk running into one of Lady Gabi's coconspirators? I doubt she worked alone," Remington said archly. He stood. "I should make sure Crowe doesn't damage my boat while he tries to dock with the yacht."

"You'll be safe in your room. I can arrange for guards to be posted in the hallway so no one else gets to you," Thorne said.

"We're even, Thorne," I snapped, unable to take his sudden interest. "I saved your life, you saved mine. You don't owe me anything else, not guards, not walking through the hallway. Nothing."

Thorne gave a half shrug. "My friends call me Alistair."

"That's nice."

"I hoped you and I could be friends," Thorne prompted.

"I thought you wanted to send me back to Nexa?"

Thorne shifted uncomfortable and glanced at the yacht. "The Seekers from Nexa destroyed my wife's home, killed her family, and took everything away from her. I hate them. I hate everyone who hurt her, but she was the one who pointed out that if I had succeeded in convincing the King to send you back to Nexa, I would have been helping the people I hate hurt another one of their victims. That was before you saved my life, and from more than the injuries of my fall."

"How did you fall?" I asked. His statement was an apology, in an indirect way, and so in an indirect way, I would accept his offer of friendship, unless he proved to be annoying.

He shook his head. "My wife and I were talking to princess Elle when there was this gust of wind. It picked me and Princess Elle up and blew us right over the edge. Elle was lucky, she's powerful enough to take her second form in practically an instant. I'm not, taking second form never even occurred to me until I had already hit the ground."

"You can fly too?" I asked.

"Sort of, not like Elle or Bramble."

"Who's Bramble?"

His grin shifted from embarrassment to gentle. "Bramble is my wife."

The woman who told him I wasn't a threat. I already liked her.

The yacht grew close enough the yacht grew close enough that Crowe was forced to slow the boat down. The back of the yacht was open, revealing a narrow space just wide enough for the boat to slip in. Remington gave Crowe careful instructions and Crowe snapped back at Remington as he gently eased the boat into the yacht.

"See, not a scratch," Crowe snipped.

"What do you want, a medal?" Remington teased. He jumped out of the boat and watched me, expectantly.

"Are you sure it's okay to leave Rowan here like this?" I asked glancing at Rowan and being incredibly careful not to stare or notice the scar that curled across his very fit chest. I seriously doubted women wanted to marry this guy simply for political advantage. That had to be a lie they told the leaders in their Houses so they could get permission to pursue Rowan.

"Crowe will stay with him. He's heavy and he's going to be sleeping like that for a while."

Belatedly, I remembered that Rowan, like me, was a telepath and if what he had just been through drained too much of his magic, he was vulnerable. I thinned out my mental wall just enough to check his wall. It was intact, but far too thin and frayed.

"Wait a minute," I said to Alistair and Remington. I knelt next to Rowan and gently put my fingers on his temple, the physical connection helped me focus on what I was about to attempt.

If telepaths trusted each other, it was possible for one to tamper with the mental barrier of another. I gently let my magic flow over his wall. When he didn't resist, I set to work. I fed my magic into his wall, strengthening it. As I did so, I expected my magic to drain, it wasn't easy to build up another's mental defenses, but when I was done, I had *more* magic.

I used thin strands of my healing magic to make sure I didn't somehow siphon Rowan's magic.

But no.

Rowan's magic was still low, but no lower than it had been. If anything, his reserves were rapidly replenishing now that his wall was repaired and wasn't pulling his magic.

"Hope, it's normal for dragons to sleep after switching back and forth between first and second form. He is fine."

"Right," I said, shaking my head. "Yeah, of course he's fine."

He was fine, but the question was, was I? Magic didn't replenish as it was being used, just the opposite, it replenished in rest and calm. I should be every bit as exhausted as Rowan after healing my own injuries then fixing his mental wall, to say nothing of the effort taken to not die at the bottom of the ocean. Instead, I felt wired, jittery, and ready to perform any feat of magic, no matter how large. At least my teeth didn't change again.

I climbed out of the boat and followed Remington through the boat, with Alistair trailing behind me.

When we reached my cabin, there was a guard already stationed outside my door.

"Thank you, Adalind,"

Adalind nodded and stepped away from the door.

I expected my room to be empty. Instead, there were three people in the room. Athena, Amara, and a woman I didn't recognize. She wasn't wearing any kind of uniform, but the kind of casual clothes Rowan vetoed me bringing on this trip. Her hair was braided in a thick swirl of cornrows she was nervously twisting into a bun at the nape of her neck.

"That took longer than anticipated," Amara commented.

"Hope, why are you all wet, again?" Athena demanded. She looked at my dress with disgust.

"Hope fell in the ocean," Remington said quickly.

"Let me find you some clean clothes," the woman said. She stood and went to the closet.

"You don't have to do that miss... um.... Lady.... I'm sorry who are you?"

"My name is Bramble. I am Athena's instructor," she said,

completely ignoring my objection as she fished another dress out of my closet then started rummaging for underwear.

I glanced at Alistair. "Your wife?"

He nodded and grinned.

"Here, take these into the bathroom and change." She sniffed loudly then glared at me. "Take a shower while you're in there."

"Thanks," I said sarcastically. I went into the bathroom and quickly did as she instructed. As I washed my hair, I found feathers tangled in my hair near my scalp. I pulled them out and set them by the sink, unnerved by the discovery, and more so by the realization that my hair, once chin length, had grown six inches.

As soon as I was dressed, I stepped out into the room. I was lucky, the only person missing was Remington. I smiled wanly at Athena, then motioned frantically to Amara.

Amara climbed off the bed she was lounging on as she spoke to Bramble and took the four steps it took to reach me.

"Come in here," I hissed. I pulled her into the bathroom and shut the door,

"It's cramped in here," she said, looking around. "Why is your bathroom so small?"

"That's not important." I grabbed the feathers and held them up. "These were in my hair, and my hair *grew* and instead of having less magic after healing, I have more!" I hissed. I kept my voice low, but only just.

Amara's eyes widened slightly. "You sound like these changes are unexpected."

I scoffed. "Of course, these changes are unexpected!"

"Destiny did not explain?" Amara asked tentatively.

"Who is Destiny? What are you talking about?" I demanded.

"Destiny, Destiny," Amara said.

"Her name is Destiny?"

"No," Amara tapped the mirror and the reflection shifted to an image of a woman. "This is Destiny. Perhaps she used an alias on Nexa?"

I studied the image of the woman. Her skin was the same

gold hue brown as mine, and her hair was black. I used to dye my hair black and pluck my eyebrows into the same arch. I used to wear the same dark makeup, although I switched to brighter colors when I came to Valoria. It was creepy, how much Megaera molded my appearance after this woman.

"I've never seen this woman," I said uncomfortably.

Amara groaned. "Well, I'm pretty new at this too. I'll...I'll contact...I'll contact Logan. He'll train you, I'm sure." She nodded to herself and slicked back her hair nervously.

"What are talking about?" I snapped.

"Okay," Amara nodded again and stepped back.

"Enchanter Logan trained me. He can train you."

"Amara," I said slowly. "What. Is. Happening. To. Me?"

"Ok, have you heard of the enchanters and enchantresses?"

"No."

Amara sighed and leaned against the door. "Then I'll start from the beginning. Centuries ago, a ship of survivors from a distant planet found refuge on a planet. These refugees were nearly immortal, and became known as enchanters, and their children became leaders among the residents of that world. When danger came to the world the residents were forced to flee, and the enchanters eventually determined it was time to pass on their unique magic to a new generation. Through the centuries, when a child is born worthy to inherit an enchanter's power, the previous enchanter passes on their power, and gives up their immortality. I am the Enchantress of Love. You are the Enchantress of Loyalty, although I confess, I didn't recognize you as such until your powers woke, which apparently happened today."

Enchantress of Love? Enchantress of Loyalty? "Megaera, my insane grandmother, was worshiped as a Goddess on Nexa. The Goddess of Life. She thought I was the Goddess of War. It almost sounds like you are advocating for the same insanity I left on Nexa." My voice was flat, and I glared at her, expecting her to deny the statement, to somehow clarify.

"I don't know who the Enchanter or Enchantress of Life is, although I was taught, they are the most powerful of all of us.

Goddess isn't quite the right word, although we are referred to as such."

"No," I interrupted. I opened the door. "Get out. Get out and stay away from me."

"Hope, you asked, I can help you understand what's happening."

"Get away from me, and don't contact me again."

Amara nodded slowly and walked out of the bathroom, and past everyone still lingering in my room.

"What was that about?" Athena asked.

I sat on the bed next to her and glanced at Alistair and Bramble, but they were just as bewildered as Athena.

"Just as disagreement, nothing to worry about." I examined the screen in her lap.

"Math again?"

"If you're alright, we should get going," Bramble said.

"I'm fine," I said. I wasn't really, but I also wasn't up to entertaining strangers.

"I'm good," Athena said. "Although Hope is a total hypocrite. Did you know she wouldn't let me balance on the ramp because she didn't want me to fall in the water and have to get rescued by my dad? Then she goes and jumps into the water."

Alistair grinned. "Hope is a little reckless."

"Thanks," I deadpanned.

Alistair grinned and led Bramble out of the room.

"Is Dad truly, okay?" Athena asked.

"He's fine, just tired," I assured her.

"So why do we have to stay in here?" Athena asked.

"It's just for tonight," I tried. "How about I help you with your math homework?"

"Yeah. Why is it so easy for you?" Athena asked.

"Math is logic, it follows strict rules. You just follow the rules to get the answer." I read through the instructions and examples twice before I found where Athena was struggling. When dinner came, it was from a guard, and when no word from Rowan came after dinner, Athena eventually settled on the extra bed and fell asleep.

As it grew later, I realized I was still too wired to sleep, and too anxious to be distracted by my screen. Still, when the knock came on my door, I about jumped out of my skin.

I opened the door, assuming it was the guard, but it was Rowan. His hair was still damp and fell in his face in a messy tangle.

"Rowan, Athena's asleep," I whispered as I let him in.

"Is she okay?" he whispered back.

"Yeah, she's okay, worried about you."

He nodded and looked at Athena, curled up away from us and gently snoring.

"I asked them to bring her here, I thought it would be easier to secure one location instead of two. I'll take her back to our rooms."

I shook my head. "Let her sleep. I don't mind." I sat down on the bench and leaned against the wall. "Are you sure you're alright?"

Rowan scoffed and sat down on the bench next to me. "Lady Gabi is from one of the more persistent Houses seeking an alliance with the House of Argentia. I didn't want to risk offending her, so I never refused her outright. I should have. I'm sorry."

I shook my head. "How long do you have to find a bride?"

Rowan sighed and looked at the bed where Athena lay. "It's custom for discussions for arranged marriages to begin when a noblewoman turns ten. My mother expects me to have a bride to help me with those discussions for Athena. If not, I will marry who my mother chooses. That was the deal I made eight years ago. Back then, I thought eight years was plenty of time to find some-one, but I still haven't, and I'm running out of time."

"What are you looking for in a partner?" I asked. I grinned at him and tried to turn it into a joke. "Maybe I could help you find someone for real, so you aren't stuck with your mother's choice."

"She means well, but if she had her way, I'd follow centuries of tradition," he rolled his eyes, a gesture that surprised me.

"Rowan, what do you want?" I repeated, more gently this

time.

He sighed. "For my daughter to not have an arranged marriage. She doesn't want to be a Lady in either court. She wants to be a royal companion. But she's a firstborn, and I need to marry someone who will support that level of deviation from what's expected."

"Or you could just not marry, not make your daughter marry, let her do what she wants with her life and tell anyone who expects otherwise to go chew on excrement," I said with a shrug. "This isn't a dictatorship, I think if all you have to worry about is the opinions of your peers, you should stop caring what they think."

"It's a little more complicated than that," Rowan said with a chuckle. "That's a disgusting analogy, by the way."

"It's disgusting that people expect you to marry so you can force your daughter to marry. No one should be forced to live the life they don't want." I turned my arm, to look at the flawless healed skin.

Rowan took my hand. I glanced up at him. He was closer than I realized and slowly leaned in. I froze. It wasn't possible. I denied what was happening until his lips pressed against mine in a gentle kiss. I leaned against him and kissed him back, deepening the kiss into something more passionate than either of us intended.

Rowan pulled back, reluctantly. "Hope…"

I leaned forward, and when he didn't flinch away, I gently pressed my lips against the corner of his mouth in a soft peck. "We'll be okay tonight. Go, get some rest," I whispered. I didn't want him to tell me whatever he was struggling to say. I didn't want to hear that this was an impossible match, that he needed to marry some noble girl from a respectable House, and we couldn't ever kiss like that again. These were things I knew, but for one night, I wanted to have the untarnished memory of that kiss.

I pulled away, and Rowan slowly nodded, content to leave things unsaid. He stood and walked out of the room, pausing only to talk to the guard before the door shut.

I curled up on the bed opposite of Athena's and tried to direct my thoughts away from freezing water or the inevitability of Rowan's rejection.

# Chapter Six

The next morning, the guard followed me and Athena to the dining room after informing us that they were confident they had arrested all who conspired with Lady Gabi. He thought it was safe to traverse the yacht, but at least one guard would stay with us just in case. Athena was quick to ask if that meant her lessons were suspended, a dream that was shattered when I informed her that I would accompany her to her lessons, so she wouldn't miss anything. I doubted there would be much chance for leisure on this trip anyway, so the very least I could do was limit the disruption to Athena's life.

The guard wouldn't sit at the table with us, so I sat next to Athena and glanced at the empty side of the table.

"Where's Rowan?" I asked.

Athena glared at me like I was stupid. "He took *second* form yesterday, without the right charms and preparations. He's probably going to sleep all day today, at least. I once took second form, to prove I could, and I was in bed for a week. If you don't do it right, it's hard."

"He came to check on you last night, he looked tired, but not 'stay in bed all day' tired," I argued.

Athena smirked at tried to hide a laugh. "Um, that called faking it, it's an old survival technique. Never show how weak you are until you're dead. Trust me, he's going to be sleeping today. Which sucks because I always hang out with him during the Dusk Dance."

"What's that?" I asked.

"It's this dance the women and girls do on the deck…" she paused and studied me. "Would you take me?"

"Are you allowed to go to the dance?" I asked, raising an eyebrow.

Athena scoffed. "Of course! But it's no fun to go by yourself."

"Don't you have friends?" I asked as a server set plates of steaming, foamy bread in front of us.

"I have classmates. People I get along with in lessons, but not friends to go to dances with."

"Why not?" I asked. I turned my focus on her. Athena was sarcastic and bossy, but also funny and interesting and not malicious. Surely, she could find a friend or two.

Athena slumped in her chair and poked at her bread. "I have male friends, but the other girls think I'm weird. All they want to talk about is their marriage negotiations. I'm a couple of levels ahead, so the girls are older, and I guess that's all that matters."

"Not really," I said, remembering Rowan's resolve to not force Athena into an arranged marriage. Then something occurred to me.

"Athena, if marriages are arranged when you're a child, why are there available women trying to marry your father? Wouldn't they be married already?"

This time Athena laughed. "Those are the women who either turned down their arranged spouse or were turned down. The marriages are arranged early, but if you don't like the person, you can always say no. There was a revolution to win that right." She stuck her chin up defiantly. "If my stepmother tries to arrange a marriage for me, I'm going to say no."

I recalled the sad look in Rowan's eyes when he told me defiance wasn't so simple. I wondered if the right was there, but the pressure to agree wasn't any less. It made sense in a sick sort of way to agree. After all, if the marriages were arranged exclusively by parents, and everyone made the negotiations when the children were still young, who knew what sort of person they would be paired with next time?

I took a slow bite of my food, starving but no longer in the mood to eat.

"Hope," Elle sat down on the opposite side of the table and smiled nervously at me. "My husband told me what happened yesterday. Are you alright?"

"Just a little waterlogged," I joked.

"I'm sorry this happened," Elle shook her head. "There will be a trial in a few days, but I've already dismissed Gabi as my companion. I suspected she wouldn't work out, but I never suspected she was capable of murder."

I shrugged.

Elle took a deep breath and looked at me. "Hope, do you know what a companion is?"

I glanced at Athena. Rowan had mentioned Athena was interested in becoming a Royal Companion, but I hadn't thought to ask what that meant at the time. Athena's gaze was focused on Elle.

"I don't know what it means," I confessed.

"In the D'Valoria House, it is custom for the heir to the throne to be assigned a companion at birth, someone who is both protector and confidant. My husband's companion is Crowe. They grew up together. When I married, the King asked me to choose a companion and suggested Gabi because of her valuable connections. However, I spoke with the King this morning and he agreed that a different message should be sent with my choice in companion."

"Why are you telling me this?" I asked. It wasn't like I was some valuable member of the nobility here; she didn't need to placate me.

Elle took a deep breath. "I wish to send a message to Lady Gabi's allies. I want to make it clear that I will not in any form support or condone her behavior."

I still wasn't sure that that had to do with me.

Elle smiled and adjusted her hair, somehow, with a gentle tug, she managed to get the entire elaborate mass of braids and curls piled on her head straight. I was immediately envious. I wish

I could fix a bun so easily when it skewered.

"I think the best message would be to show my unwavering support of her intended victim. As a refugee, you are easily dismissed in the minds of Lady Gabi's peers. As my companion, you wouldn't be so easily ignored."

"And why exactly would you want a refugee as a companion?" I asked. I could see the benefit in the trial, but she was asking for something far more long term.

Elle sat up a little straighter. "Two reasons, the first I've already explained, but second, I'm curious as to what insight you will bring. Lord Rowan tells me you are intelligent, creative, and honest. Those are valuable qualities to me."

I glanced at Athena.

"Do it," she whispered, her eyes wide. This was her dream, to become a royal companion. If I accepted, I could learn the role, and teach it to her.

"What does a companion do? What are the expectations?"

Elle nodded once, accepting my curiosity as acceptance. "You will come with me to meetings. At first, I want you to be silent and listen, observe. Offer you opinions to me in private."

I nodded. That sounded easy, and obvious. I could make myself look stupid in a meeting with an ignorant comment, and Elle would look equally foolish for putting me in such a trusted position.

"What else?" I asked.

"For now, just that. Crowe will arrange for you to learn some basic combat skills."

I nodded. I was curious to see how my training compared to the combat skills taught here.

"Well, when do I start?" I asked.

"Yes," Athena hissed. At least someone was thrilled with my new role.

"When we return to the capital. I will have my aid send you, my schedule. Do you have plans for the rest of today and tomorrow?"

"I will be accompanying Athena to her lessons. Rowan

thought we would be safer together."

Elle turned to Athena. "Will I see the two of you at the Dusk Dance tonight?"

"If Dad wakes up long enough to tell Hope it's okay if I go. I shouldn't have told her I've never gone before," Athena said sullenly.

Elle giggled. "Well, if Lord Rowan gives permission, I'll see you both tonight. I won't keep you." She stood and gave a slight curtsy before leaving.

After breakfast, I followed Athena to the deck where Bramble sat with a small group of older kids. After explaining why, I was there, I settled a short distance away and listened as Bramble began her lesson.

Once the lesson began, I soon found myself lost, then bored.

I checked my screen, and found a document sent from one of Elle's aids. The document outlined the expected code of conduct for a Princess's Companion, as well as the dress code, and the compensation, which included rooms of my own in the building, and enough money to live comfortably even after the temporary position was done. I could learn a good trade, and with a favorable reference from the royal family, I could work anywhere on Karabeeya.

For the rest of Athena's lessons, I read through the document carefully. Apparently, when Rowan said every detail of my appearance meant something in the courts, he wasn't joking. A new wardrobe would be sent to my room, there was a note clarifying that I wasn't to move to my new rooms until after the investigation was completed and Gabi's stuff moved out, and when I was on duty, there were rules on jewelry, makeup, clothing, and behavior. Fortunately, it was extensive, but easy enough to learn.

When lessons were done, Athena ran to me, ignoring her classmates' attempts to get her attention.

"Dad hasn't responded yet, let's go check on him."

She rushed to the stairs, forcing me to rush after her, a difficult feat as the yacht lurched on the waves.

I thought Rowan's rooms would be like Gabi's, with the bedroom separated from the living area so I didn't hesitate to follow Athena into the room. It was a rash choice I regretted as soon as I saw Rowan asleep on a bench.

Athena poked her father repeatedly until he slowly shifted to face her and wearily opened his eyes.

"Can I go to the Dusk Dance with Hope?" she asked loudly.

"Of course, you can," Rowan grumbled.

"Great, I'm going to go change," Athena skipped to her room, leaving me alone with Rowan.

He noticed me and sat up.

I studied him. His exhaustion was apparent. If anything, he seemed more exhausted than last night. I thinned my mental wall and checked his, surprised when I felt his exhaustion coupled with curiosity and attraction. I quickly poured more magic into his wall, then retreated behind my own, ensuring it was strong enough to completely block out all thoughts and emotions, and keep my own safely concealed.

"Thank you," he said, glancing up at me.

"You're weaker," I said. I sat down next to him. "Should I call a healer?"

Rowan shook his head. "I'm all right, I just didn't sleep very well on this bench."

"Then why didn't you go to your bed?" I asked archly.

"It didn't seem to be worth the effort," he admitted. "How did you convince Athena to go to the dance?"

I shrugged. "She asked me."

Rowan ran his hand through his messy hair and nodded, then slumped down.

"Okay, let's get you to your bed," I said firmly. When Rowan didn't move, I leaned down and gave him a quick kiss, purely to startle him into a little more alertness and of course for no other motivation.

The kiss worked. He jerked up and I used the opportunity to pull him to his feet.

Then it was his turn to surprise me. He wrapped his arms around me in a tight embrace, and fortunately I was tall and strong or inheriting his sudden weight would have knocked me over.

He rested his head on my shoulder, his face buried in my hair as he took sharp, trembling breaths.

"I love you," he whispered.

I clutched him tightly for a second euphoric before reality came crashing through my head with the force of a tsunami. What did I think such a confession meant? That with my new job suddenly I'd be good enough to marry one of the wealthiest nobles on Karabeeya? That he would sacrifice his reputation and opportunities for better alliances for worthless me?

I gently pushed him away from me and took his arm over my shoulder so I could continue to support his weight.

"Get some sleep, before you really do need a healer," I said as I pulled him toward the other door. I made it into the room and dumped him on the bed before I turned around and walked out of the room, ignoring his exhausted attempts to call my name.

He loved me, but I wished he kept his that fact to himself. It would have been easier to nurse my own broken heart on his wedding day if I could have convinced myself that my love was one sided.

"Hope, what do you think?" Athena spun around. The silver dress had a voluminous skirt and over the whole thing was a sheer layer embroidered with stars. The dress had a high collar, and off the shoulder sleeves that were held in place with a star-studded ribbon. She held a bag of crystal stars in her hand. When she stopped twirling, she glared up at me with worry.

"Are you crying?"

I wiped my face quickly. I hadn't even realized the tears were there.

"I'm, a little overwhelmed. But you look beautiful."

"The stars go in my hair," she hesitated.

"Help me pick out a dress, and I'll help you with your hair," I offered.

Athena grinned and opened the door.

"By the time we're ready, it will be time for the dance to

start!"

Athena was a little too enthusiastic. By the time we were ready, and, on the deck, the party had not yet started, and the sound system was still being tested. We sat at a small table out of the way to wait.

I toyed with the tiny braids tucked behind my ear. Those loyal to the future queen above all others wore some kind of braid in their hair, as a visible sign of their loyalty. I wasn't used to the tiny braids yet, although I did like them. My dress was shorter, the perfect length and looseness for any physical activity, since I wasn't sure what kind of dances were involved in the Dusk Dance.

"When do you start?" Athena asked. "Being the champion for the Princess?"

"When we return to the city, there's a ceremony at a park, which will be my first event."

"Are you excited?" Athena asked.

I nodded. "It will be different," I said. "I don't know how much I will like it. I've never even seen a companion."

"A companion is the caretaker and confidante of their royal. Think of yourself as Princess Estelle's friend first."

"Caretaker too?" I asked.

"Okay, so companions are chosen for the royal when they are born. The companion helps raise the royal. I guess that wouldn't apply with you."

The dance opened with a lighthearted speech. Everyone at the dance was female, no boys allowed. The music was loud, fast, and encouraged chaotic dancing. I stayed with Athena, and when she finally showed signs of exhaustion, I took her back to her room.

Luckily, Rowan was still asleep.

# Chapter Seven

My first night back in Veritas was a relief. I locked myself in my room. Tomorrow. Tomorrow I would confront Rowan. It was a mistake to kiss, and a greater one for me to kiss him, especially when Athena caught us. He would be relieved to know I expected nothing, he would understand how right it was that I leave his family alone and seek accommodations elsewhere until the companion rooms were available.

Eager to take my mind off the spiraling depressing nature of those thoughts, I walked over to Millenia's book of prophecies, and stopped. The book flipped open on its own and the pages flipped rapidly before settling open.

I approached the creepy book and read the passage.

*To free a dragon from the treason curse:*

*Dragons from Talaraine lose themselves when they take second and third forms, but there is a way to partially restore their sanity.*

*First, one must get close enough to demonstrate complete trust. Resting one's forehead against the dragon, or a kiss on the cheek is sufficient. With this demonstration of trust, implant the telepathic command for freedom, a simple command that the dragon belongs to no one.*

*If successful, the dragon will revert to first form, and can maintain limited sentience in second or third form when close to the telepath who freed them with the same efficiency as proximity to an active Wyvernite crystal.*

*You have the strength to do this, my daughter. Not many telepaths do.*

I closed the book and stepped away from it. Two things freaked me out, first the Book *moved on its own*. And second, the realization that Millenia knew from the start that I could use telepathy to implant suggestions and commands in the mind of another, and somehow managed to love me anyway.

Sleep did not come easily that night, and dawn, and with it the coming distractions, was a welcome relief.

I dressed with frequent verification against the dress code for a companion and left before Rowan or Athena left their rooms.

It was the first time I rode the elevator to the top floors. Previously, the royal floors were off limits, but part of my duties as companion was to ensure my royal was ready and on time.

I made my way to Elle's personal rooms, but they were empty. Unwilling to go into her bedroom, which seemed rude, I sent her a message.

Seconds later, Elle waltzed into the room, completely ready for the day.

"I thought I was supposed to wake you up?" I said, holding up my screen with the document still on it.

Elle paused. "I think that document is overly generalized. We will figure this out together."

I had no objection to one less requirement. To the annoyance of the guards, Elle wanted to get to the park early, to walk some of the quiet paths before the ceremony. This apparently meant extra work, and extra guards to quickly secure the paths she wanted to walk.

"Okay, who wants you dead so badly?" I asked after the arrangements were made and we were finally on our way to the park.

Elle hesitated. "My marriage represents the first time a ground dragon in the royal family has married a sky dragon. It simply has never been done. A few years ago, significant resources were expended to find a new home for the sky dragons, but it didn't work out. There are some who think that was still the best and only real option. To those people, my marriage to Remington represents a threat to that possibility and a threat to the current status quo."

"Then why go to the park?" I asked.

"I will not be held hostage by a miniscule percentage of the population simply because their hatred is loud. I will not cower. They will learn to adjust to change, or at least accept that the change is inevitable."

The car parked; we followed the assigned guards from the car to the garden path Elle wanted to see. The guards hung back, giving her and me a little privacy.

"These flowers remind me of my childhood home," Elle said, brushing her hand over a cluster of flickering orange flowers.

An unexpected shadow passed over us, I looked up, then was thrown to the side with a blast from behind us.

A bush broke my fall, and I broke Elle's.

"Are you hurt?" Elle asked as she scrambled off me.

"No," I groaned. The bush wasn't a comfortable landing, but I fared far better than the guards that were next to the blast. It didn't look like there were any survivors.

The shadow passed over us again. This time I saw the creature that cast it. Humanoid, vaguely. He had wings that grew out of his back, deformed feet, and fine fur that covered him. The creature swept over us again, I shoved Elle, pushing her away from the creature before he could snatch her up.

The next time the creature swooped down, I grabbed a rock, imbued it with a small charge of my magic, and threw the rock at the creature. As anticipated, he avoided the rock, but it still exploded close enough to the creature for the blast to knock him out of the air and momentarily disorient him.

I sprinted to him and fell to my knees next to him. I pressed my head against his, and reluctantly lowered my wall. The creature's thoughts were chaotic, ill formed, and overwhelmed by a foreign directive to kill Elle. I focused on that foreign directive, sloppily forced onto his mind by an overeager telepath with brute force and none of the finesse required to make such a command stay in a rational mind.

I burned the command away and implanted a command of my own.

"Keep your mind, no matter your form, Dragon," I whispered.

I lost my balance then, the exhaustion complete and overwhelming. I fell to the ground next to the creature, which gave me an odd and up-close view as his wings faded away, and the fur on his arms, chest, and face fell off his skin in a mess around him. His hair was less thick, and it no longer covered his face.

My wall flickered, too weak to block out his relief, or Elle's worry.

"He's okay now, won't hurt anyone," I gasped, my words slurred. I looked at the dragon as he sat up and put his hands above his head.

Hate. Rage. Suspicion. I could sense it overwhelmingly in the guards that surrounded us. I tried to sit up, but stars exploded in my vision, and I fell back to the ground, unaware of anything else.

# Chapter Eight

When I woke, it was to the gentile sound of a stylus scratching on a screen. I opened my eyes and felt the soft, plush, familiar feel of my new bed. I turned my head, it was all I could manage without throwing up, and saw Rowan sitting in the chair near my bed. As usual, he was working.

"How long?" I asked. My throat was dry, and my voice was cracked and high pitched.

"Here," Rowan stood up and slipped an ice chip in my mouth. I sucked on it, grateful for the cold.

"You slept all of yesterday and the entire night. I just sent Athena to her classes."

I struggled to sit up. Judging from the dark circles under his eyes, and the sickly pallor of his skin, I guessed he hadn't slept at all.

"Did you stay with me all night?" I asked, torn between creeped out and touched.

"I recalled your reluctance to be alone when your mental defenses shielding your telepathy was down. Was that incorrect?"

"No, thank you, you're very kind," I said. I swung my legs over the side of the bed and took a deep breath. Once I was no longer moving, the dizziness wasn't so terrible.

"What happened after I passed out?" I asked without moving.

"Your new friend was arrested, although, both Elle and

Remy insisted he be held here in the building. Elle was insistent that thanks to you, he was no longer a threat."

"He's not my friend," I said quickly. "I just… knew what was wrong. He was being manipulated by a telepath on top of whatever madness he was suffering in that form. I'm guessing he's a Talarainian dragon?"

Rowan nodded. "I have not had the chance to speak to him, but that is what Elle reported. Apparently, now that he is in first form, he is adamant that he is no longer a threat, and he wishes to speak to you. Statements Elle has confirmed are truths."

"Why does he want to talk to me?" I asked.

"Well, actually, he requested to speak to 'the gorgeous babe with white striped hair,' but I assume that he's referring to you, and you seem to have a fan."

"I'm taken," I said without thought.

"By whom?" Rowan asked quickly, and with more anger than my idiotic slip warranted.

I tensed then smirked at Rowan. "If you have to ask, you won't get the answer," I wasn't going to admit he was my soulmate, especially if he was going to marry for political advantage. "I'm hungry and I feel gross. Give me a few minutes, then do you have time to go with me to meet this dragon?"

Rowan stood and nodded stiffly. "I'll wait for you in my office," he walked out of the room.

"Thank you," I shouted after him with a grin he didn't see.

Once I was ready, and after I ate a quick meal, I found Rowan in his office. He shut off his screen as soon as he noticed me lurking in the doorway and stood.

"Is it alright if Remy and Elle accompany us? The King has entrusted them to determine the future of this dragon."

I shrugged, indifferent to the plan. "Do we know this dragon's name?" I asked.

"I don't know anything more than I already told you. He seems mostly intent on wanting to speak to you and assuring us he is no threat despite his initial attack on the princess," Rowan said as he led the way to the elevator. The elevator took us to a lower floor, but not as low as the holding cell I was kept in when I first arrived at this building. The hallway was similar to the layout of Rowan's floor, although Rowan didn't have several guards stationed throughout his hallway. Remy and Elle stood at the end of the hallway, near a door with two guards, in addition to their bodyguards. Crowe stood to the side of the royal couple, next to Aaron.

"Hope heard you knocked out a dragon in second form with nothing more than an exploding rock," Crowe called.

"Something like that."

"Crowe," Aaron, a guard assigned to Elle, and Crowe's little brother, hissed.

"What? I'm impressed," Crowe said.

"How many of us are going to be talking to the dragon?" Rowan interrupted.

"It looks like there will be six of us, but don't worry, the room is plenty big," Crowe said. He tapped gently on the door.

The door swung open, and the dragon stuck his head out into the hallway. As soon as he saw me, he grinned with goofy excitement.

"It's you! You're here!"

"We came to talk to you," I said, uncomfortable by his excitement. "Is it okay if we come into the room?"

"All of you?" he asked with a nervous glance at all the guards in the hallway.

"Just six of us, we have questions," I said quickly.

The dragon nodded slowly. He opened the door the rest of the way and stepped to the side to let us in.

His rooms were similar to mine, consisting of a large sitting room, a small kitchen, and likely a bedroom and bathroom, although I couldn't see those rooms because the doors were shut. He sat down in a chair, leaving the curved benches for the rest of us. Aaron and Crowe stood on either side of the room. I sat down between Rowan and Remy, with Elle on Remy's other side.

"So...Do you have a name?" I asked in the awkward silence.

"You can call me Tatsu," the dragon said brightly.

"Do you have a real name?" Rowan asked, unimpressed.

"Tatsu works," he said with a shrug. "What are your names?" When he asked, he was only looking at me.

"I'm Hope, this is Crown Prince Remington of the Royal House of D'Valoria, his wife, Crown Princess Estelle of the Royal House of D'Valoria," I moved my hand to indicated Rowan. "This is my friend, Lord Rowan of the Noble House of Argentia, and these are the prince's and princess's bodyguards, Crowe and Aaron of the House of Annise."

"What House are you from, Hope? Nobility? Royalty? Dragon? Novem?" Tatsu asked.

I shook my head. "I don't belong to a House, I'm a rogue," I said simply. I wasn't going to explain my past to this stranger. "What about you?"

"I come from the House of Avalon. It's a dragon House on Talaraine." Tatsu said.

"I figured you were from Talaraine," I said proud of my correct guess.

"I'm interested in learning how you got from Talaraine to Karabeeya and ended up under the control of a telepath?" Remy said.

"I've never been to Talaraine," Tatsu said. "But I'll tell you me story, if you really want it."

"Yeah," I prompted.

"My mother was kidnapped from Talaraine and brought to a Poltron work camp on Karabeeya. It sucked, but she adjusted to life in the work camp as people do. She met someone and had me. I was born in that work camp, it's always been my home, until some time ago, I don't know how long, a woman came and gathered a group of us. We were kept in small cages and…" he winced and trailed off, lost in a particularly painful memory.

I knew what he didn't want to say. There was a process to break down a person, so a telepath could more easily control them. Given how sloppy the command I removed had been placed in Tatsu's mind, I guessed Tatsu had to be completely worn down with physical and psychological torture.

"What happened after the cages?" I asked, giving him an opportunity to not talk about that particular experience with six strangers.

"The woman came, and she…was in my head. She wanted me to kill someone," he glanced at Elle. "You, actually… sorry about that… then she wanted me to take second form. I did, I didn't have a choice, I couldn't control it, or anything else I did. He turned his attention to me. "You saved me, both from the woman and getting executed here."

I shrugged. "I just dismantled the command and replaced it with one of my own. My command should shield you from further control."

Tatsu nodded. "I remember it. You made it so I would always know my own mind. Do you think its strong enough to override the curse inflicted on all Talarainian Dragons? Would I be able to take Final Form and maintain my sanity?"

"Let's not test that," Rowan said quickly.

"Especially not in the city," Remy added.

Tatsu glanced at me. "I'm in your debt, Hope, I owe you, my life."

"Such words are best not spoken lightly," Rowan warned.

"I speak to them knowing full well what they mean," Tatsu responded. He looked at me, expectant, and nervous. He was waiting for something, but I had no idea what.

I glanced at Rowan, hoping for some clue as to what Tatsu wanted.

Rowan took pity on me and leaned over to whisper in my ear. "He owes you a life debt. The proper thing to do is accept. Please don't refuse. There is no greater insult, and he will take his own life to repay the debt if you refuse."

"What?" I hissed, drawing everyone's startled attention.

"I mean, I accept?" I said quickly.

"We still need to determine exactly what kind of threat you are," Remy interrupted.

"Whoa! I'm not a threat! Hope fixed that. I swear I won't hurt Princess Ally-Sandy."

"Ally-Sandy?" I asked.

He flushed, his face and neck red with embarrassment. "I forgot her name."

"Alexandra," Lexie said. She sighed and looked at Remy. "He speaks the truth."

"Do you have any other implanted commands?" Remy asked.

Tatsu shrugged. "I'm not exactly an expert in implanted commands."

I hissed, reluctant. "I am." After years of not using my telepathy for implanted commands, I was going to use it twice in less than two days, and I already established I had no stamina for it. I was going to be asleep for another full day.

I stood up and moved to the chair where Tatsu sat. I sat on the table near his chair and rested my forehead against his.

His mind was open, without any resistance. He trusted me, simply because I saved his life. I tried to skip over his memories, although that was impossible. I couldn't ignore them all, but I could focus on my goal, searching for foreign commands. Eventually, I could confidently say there were no lingering commands.

I pulled away from him. "He's fine," I said as slumped. "Your highnesses, if it's alright, I'd like to go back to my bed."

"Tatsu, will you answer the rest of your questions without Hope present?" Elle asked.

Tatsu glanced uncertainly at me. I nodded encouragingly. I didn't want to stick around, and there was no point in having him wait until I was recovered, the sooner he proved he was trustworthy, the better for Tatsu.

"Yeah, I'll answer all of your questions," he said sullenly.

"Hope, I'll take you back home," Rowan said. He helped me stand and walked with me slowly out of the room and back to the elevator.

"Shouldn't you be listening so you can advise Remy or whatever it is you do?" I asked as soon as it occurred to me. I sat down on the elevator floor and rested against the wall.

"I prefer to hear firsthand accounts, when possible, but

truthfully, Remy can handle this." He didn't slump, let alone sit on the floor like I did, but I could sense his exhaustion. When the elevator stopped on our floor, he helped me stand. I went straight to my bed and curled up under the blanket.

Rowan sank into his chair. I looked at him for a moment, chewing my lip as I studied his stiff posture and pale face. I didn't want to be alone while I was too weak to fight off a telepathic attack, but I couldn't force him to stay up for hours when he so clearly needed sleep.

"Rowan," I paused, unsure of what to say. Finally, I scooted to the far side of the huge bed and patted the mattress next to me. "There's plenty of room, you should rest."

Rowan hesitated, but only for a brief, uncomfortable moment. He quickly made a decision and took his shoes off. He climbed into the bed, as far from me as possible. He turned his back to me. With reluctance I didn't want to admit, even to myself, I did the same and drifted to sleep.

# Chapter Nine

My dreams were discordant, a disturbing mix of Tatsu's memories and my own. I ran through a deserted work camp, chased by Megaera. I tripped over the broken body of my cousin Kayda.

"It's your doing," Megaera said mockingly.

I stared down at Kayda, at the blood flowing freely from the side of her face, where her ear used to be. In my hand, I held the bloody, ceremonial knife.

"What makes you think you can help anyone, when you cause harm as freely as I do?"

"Hope."

I tensed and opened my eyes. I expected the work camp, not the dark bedroom, or the hand on my shoulder. I turned to Rowan. He wrapped his arm around me, and I settled against his chest, without thinking, or worrying about what his actions meant to him or me.

"It was a nightmare, Hope," he said gently.

I took a deep breath. He smelled like wood, fruit, and amber. It was likely his cologne, or some expensive soap, but it was comforting just the same. He rested his cheek against mine. I should have pulled away. This wasn't what I was after when I offered to let him sleep in my room, but I wasn't disappointed. I knew though, even as I wrapped my arm around him, fully accepting his comforting presence, that one day I would regret this, when Rowan married, and I would have to find a way to accept seeing him with his wife. That realization brought another, that I wouldn't run again, no matter what the future on this world held. Even knowing that he would someday marry, for the benefit of the Valorian and Asea Royalty, I couldn't pull away from him. Whatever he was thinking, he wisely kept his wall strong so I couldn't read his thoughts, and he never pulled away. He fell asleep before I did.

Somehow, in my sleep, I ended up sprawled on Rowan's chest, my head tucked against his heart. I woke when he gently moved me back to my half of the bed.

"I'm sorry, but I need to get ready, and if you are up to it, so do you," Rowan said softly.

I moved to my pillow and turned away from him, the full realization of what I did struck me, closing my throat, and pressing against my chest. It was just sleep, but it was more familiarity, more *intimacy* that two friends had any right engaging in, particularly when that was all we could be, and I wanted so much more.

"Thank you for staying the night," I said awkwardly, not once letting my gaze leave the wall.

"Of course," Rowan said simply.

I heard the door shut, and that's when I risked getting out of bed. I was tired, but not so exhausted that I couldn't rebuild my mental wall, shower, and get ready for the day.

Once I was ready, I walked into the hall, and realized Rowan was waiting for me. He looked over my appearance with gentle approval.

"You're learning."

"Is this this really suitable for standing behind the princess all day?" I joked, giving a quick spin. I wore a simply dress with a clean cut, in a bright blue.

"You will be sitting, actually. We are going to a council meeting."

I didn't respond to that statement. It was probably something I should have already known. "Do you know what they decided to do with Tatsu?" I asked.

"Crowe adopted him into his House. He's going to stay with the Elite Guard for now. I think if you stay, he will as well."

Quickly, my days settled into a new routine. Every morning, I woke up far earlier than I wanted and went with Rowan to accompany Remy and Lexie for the day. Then, in the late afternoon, every day, we returned to spend the evening with Athena, taking turns helping her with her homework until it was time to work together to go over reports. I thought the paperwork would bore me, but it was a fascinating avenue to learn more about Karabeeya. When Elle found a permanent companion, perhaps I could find a job reviewing reports similar to these and creating concise summaries of the information. It was an amusing thought, who would have guessed I would choose an academic life?

As days turned to weeks and Rowan's deadline for marriage approached, I began to wonder if Elle would ever choose another companion, and when she asked me to accompany her for a walk in the gardens, I thought she finally found a permanent companion, especially when guards did not accompany us.

Elle didn't speak right away, and I wasn't diplomatic enough to find a way to tell her I was okay with no longer being her companion, particularly since I really wasn't. I enjoyed the routine, the challenge, and the time spent with Rowan.

"Hope, I'd like you to start speaking up when you have something to contribute, as Rowan does. I've found your insight to be unique and appreciated," she finally said.

"Okay," I said slowly. Then this wasn't about me losing my job, at least not yet. "You ditched your guards to tell me that?"

"No," Elle said with a nervous laugh. "I wanted to get your advice on a more personal matter. I'm pregnant."

"I don't know anything about that," I said promptly. "I've never been pregnant. I guess you should get comfortable shoes, I think feet swell during pregnancy."

"No. I...thought, well Dragons are like Novem, only soulmates could conceive."

"What? No," I said, shaking my head and working to not smile. "Soulmates are rare, at least among the Novem. If that were a condition of conception, we Novem would have died out long ago. The only requirement of conception is the…act."

"I was taught that an arranged marriage would lead to love, as strong as the soulmate bond, and only then would it be possible to conceive from the… act, as you call it."

I bit my lip, then decided to voice my suspicion. "That sounds like a story to make girls more comfortable about arranged marriages. If you don't have a child within three years, by Valoria law, either spouse can request a divorce, right?"

Elle nodded slowly.

"Basically, if you agree to an arranged marriage, you go into it thinking you'll either grow to love your spouse, or you have the option to get a divorce. By the time you realize otherwise, you already have a kid."

"I wasn't contemplating a divorce," Elle said defensively. "I am fond of Remy, and I don't mind spending every day with him, but I thought love would be more."

"I don't know," I said thoughtfully. "My mother used to tell stories of soulmates. She said that beyond the initial attraction and passion, love, even that love, was work that took effort and time."

Elle smiled slightly. "I've always found Remy attractive, and he's agreeable. I enjoy spending my time with him, even when it's not part of our duties."

I scratched my neck. "Pretend for a moment that the laws were different. Would you stay with him, or would you leave?"

"But the laws aren't different. We will soon have a child and we are royalty. Divorce is not an option. Blended families in the royal line are extremely frowned on. If either of us want to have a child with another person, the previous children are to be executed."

"What? Seriously?" I demanded. "I haven't seen any laws like that."

"You've been helping me with matters that affect the general population. There are three sets of laws. The general population has a set of laws. The nobility is expected to follow all of those laws, plus the rules of nobility. It's why the general population can marry who they want, but nobility is restricted to who their parents chose for them. Then there's royalty. We follow the laws of the general population, the rules of nobility, and the expectations of royalty. The expectations of royalty in Valoria don't allow for half-siblings among the royal lines. There's too much risk of dissent, and rebellion. History is filled with it. Half-siblings create split alliances, imbalances in power."

"That's cold," I said flatly. "Maybe that's the difference between Novem and Dragons, on Nexa and even in the Amaranth Empire, the view on children is completely different."

"Different in what way?" Lexie asked, startled by my vehemence.

"It's difficult for any woman to carry a Novem child to term," I said hesitantly.

"I'm well aware of the difficulty, it's another similarity between Novem and Dragons. I was taught the difficult pregnancy is due to the incredible magic in the child. I will need to start a strict regimen of herbs and medication. The regimen greatly reduces the risk. I don't know if Nexa or Amaranth has access to the regimen," Lexie said.

"There's a tea my aunt discovered that helps, but the risk is still there. For generations it's been acceptable for married couples to use surrogates. The offspring of the surrogates legally belong to the couple. They are raised as their children and the surrogate mothers have no legal rights to the children."

"When you say surrogate, do you mean mistress?" Lexie said coyly.

"Sometimes," I laughed. "Sometimes it's a mistress, sometimes it's a mutual friend of the couple, and sometimes it's a volunteer the couple never meet face to face. Adoption is also common. Mothers die," I shrugged, not finishing the comment.

"Did your birth mother die?" Lexie asked.

I shook my head. It wasn't my birth mother. "That wasn't my particular situation, and we are getting off topic. We were talking about what you want to do."

"I like Remy fine, and I could learn to love him. I guess I just feel foolish for not knowing love isn't a needed factor to get pregnant."

"We all have gaps in our educations, your highness," I said with as much excessive respect as I could muster.

My sarcasm inspired the desired response. Elle laughed, a genuine, loud, sputtering laugh that was nothing like the ladylike giggle she gave in polite company.

"Thank you for listening, Hope. I haven't spoken of my pregnancy to Prince Remy, or anyone else. I would appreciate it if he didn't hear of the pregnancy from another source."

"I will tell no one," I assured her.

Elle smiled her appreciation and moved a thing braid behind her ear. "What are your plans for the Fertility Festival?" she asked, moving on to a topic that was less stressful for her.

I stopped. "I thought I was working." The Fertility Festival was a celebration of family and children. Initially it was celebrated only in the oceans of Karabeeya, but like many of the Sea Dragon's customs, the surface countries had adopted the celebration and added to it to make it theirs.

No one in government works during the festival. You have the next three days off. Go to the celebrations, shop in the market," her smile turned wicked. "Enjoy the late-night festivities."

I smiled and considered her prompting. "Well, I suppose I could learn more about this country's customs."

Elle stepped away, back to the door to the hallway. "Fantastic. I'll see you during the festival, I'm sure."

I nodded and sat on a nearby bench. I watched Lexie leave the garden, in a considerably better mood than when we first walked. I wondered how much it bothered her that she apparently didn't love Remy. I wondered what she wanted love to feel like. Would it be simpler to have a lifelong companion chosen for me? Someone I could rely on with none of the complications of loving first without knowing if that love was ever returned.

I rode the elevator back to my floor, considering the advantages and disadvantages of not needing love to marry. Would I go willingly into an arranged marriage, despite my inconvenient feelings for Rowan? Or would I resent the match? My curiosity was moot, there was no one to arrange such a match for me, and despite living among nobility and working with them, I wasn't really one of them, my birth parents were in this solar system, but they had no idea I was still alive, and I wasn't sure if Talaraine cared about arranged marriages anyway.

The elevator door opened to a heavenly, sweet, warm smell. I took a deep breath, then followed the aroma to the main kitchen. Rowan was pulling a sheet out of one oven and swapping it for another sheet filled with neat rows of white mounds.

"You bake?" I asked, surprised.

He looked up at me, impatient. "It wasn't difficult to learn. Follow the directions and you get the right result."

"What are you baking?" I asked.

"Treasure mounds, it's for a game Athena will play tomorrow with other children in the building. There is a bauble hidden in one of the mounds. The child that finds it gets to choose the next game."

"How fun," I said. I sat on the counter and watched as he slowly and carefully created rows of the mounds on a clean sheet. When he finished, he took one of the freshly cooked mounds and handed it to me.

"Are they good?" I asked. I took the mound and examined it. It looked too white to eat, although at formal meals with the princess I often found that food was disguised to look inedible but not necessarily gross.

"Try it," Rowan prompted.

I took a bite. It was crunchy, buttery and had the crisp taste of a water fruit I usually ate with fish.

"I like this," I said, barely remembering to cover my mouth with my hand so he didn't get a view of half chewed food.

"Excellent." He moved to the next stage of his task, but I was in the way. I swallowed the last of the treasure mound and jumped off the counter as Rowan stepped to the side.

I bumped into him and put my hand on his shoulder to steady myself, but that only brought him closer. He looked into my eyes. His eyes lost their calculating look, replaced with an entirely different intensity. His gaze shifted down to my mouth, then back to my eyes before he leaned in and closed the distance between us.

"Whoa! Wait! Wait!" I shrieked. I took a step back and turned to the sink. "Just a minute, I don't want to kiss you with crumbs in my mouth." I grabbed a glass and filled it with just enough water to swish my mouth and swallow it in one gulp. "Okay, now you can kiss me if you still want to."

Rowan looked at me, bemused, but then his expression shifted to a grin, gentle and excited. He gently threaded his fingers through my hair and softly pulled my head towards his.

I expected a kiss, after all we had kissed once before, but I didn't expect the passion, the stolen breath and fiery desire that overwhelmed me as his lips moved over mine, and his hand gently clasped my back, drawing me even closer until I was pressed against him. I kissed him back, pushing against him with no other thought than to be closer still.

The door opened with a loud bang and even louder laughter. Somehow, Rowan and I managed to jump apart, and gain enough distance between us that Athena, and her unexpected companion Tatsu, couldn't possibly suspect what we had been doing only a second before.

"Hope! I found Tatsu! He said he'll help me decorate the windows for the Fertility Festival! Then when we're done, he said you could take me shopping!"

"Oh really?" I teased, even as my heart raced, and I prayed to the Rings of Aether that the amused look Tatsu was giving me, and Rowan had everything to do with his promise and nothing more.

"I need to talk to Rowan. When I told Athena, she suggested the shopping trip," Tatsu clarified.

"Ah, that makes more sense," Rowan said. "In that case, Hope, would you be willing to take Athena shopping now, and

Tatsu can help me clean up this mess?"

"Better you clean it up than me, Tatsu!" Athena yelled. She raced out of the room, ecstatic to be free of a potential chore.

"Wait, Hope, you two shouldn't go out alone," Tatsu insisted.

"The market isn't dangerous, and it's on the street in front of the building, there will be all sorts of security," Rowan objected.

"Besides, ever since Lexie was attacked," I glared at him so he would better understand I really was talking about his attack on Lexie, "I've been allowed to carry this." I unclipped a short staff, less than a foot long that was holstered to my back, just under my shirt. With a quick twist, the staff grew to its full six feet. "My father taught me how to use staff weapons, I can take care of myself... and anyone I'm responsible for." I twisted the staff again and it shrank down to its smaller size. I clipped it back in my holster and walked to the hallway where Athena was waiting.

As soon as I was out of the kitchen, I thought back to the kiss and how badly I wanted it. I couldn't make that mistake again. As much as I loved Rowan, I knew it would kill me that much more when he married. I wasn't willing to stay behind and be some silent mistress in the background. I wanted all of him, or none of him, and that was the most heartbreaking realization of all.

# Chapter Ten

"This will be perfect, Hope! Almost like shopping with a mom for the Fertility Festival!" Athena said in a rush.

I tensed, unwilling to encourage that line of thinking. "Can you settle for shopping with your buddy?" I said tentatively.

Athena bounced on her feet. "That's just as good."

"Wait, I thought the festival started tomorrow, and the market was only during the festival," I asked.

"No, the festival market opens two days before the festival and stays open for two days after, although after the festival it's more an attempt to sell what's left as fast as possible."

The elevator doors opened on the ground floor of the building. The ground floor was crowded with crowds of people. The clusters consisted of families arguing, friends laughing, and a chaotic chatter that came from every direction and was impossible to differentiate. Athena walked through the crowd. I followed, trying not to walk through families or interrupt any conversations.

I thought the market would be further away, but as soon as we left the building, we stepped into the middle of the market. Tables lined the street, decorated with bright flags, banners, and holograms that advertised their wares. There was everything from homemade jewelry to personalized services. I didn't see the connection between some of the offered goods and services, and a celebration of family and children, but I supposed this festival was an excuse to give meaningless gifts or purchase needed items for personal use.

"Flowers!" Athena yelled. She walked to the table that was overflowing with flower arrangements in beautiful vases. "Look at these flowers, Hope. This one comes in a vase with sea turtles etched in it. It's our family animal."

"Then why don't you get it for him," I said. I reached into my shirt and pulled out the medallion that I could use to pay the flower vendor.

"Flowers are bought for mothers, not fathers," the speaker was a girl a little older than Athena, who I thought took classes with her.

Athena shifted, uncomfortable. I glared at the girl, surprised that she was willing to tease Athena in front of me.

"Oh, I'm sorry. I forgot. You don't have a mother, not even a replacement because your father can't be bothered to find one for you. Really there's no reason at all for you to be looking at flower arrangements."

"Dang kid go rot in the cesspools of Aether," I snapped. "I know for a fact, men like getting flowers too." I turned to Athena. "Of course, Lord Rowan will be thrilled to get this arrangement." I turned to the vendor and held out my medallion. I earned a sizable wage as Elle's companion, and still stayed rent free in the room Rowan offered. I could easily afford it, even if Athena wanted something else to give to Rowan.

"Will this be delivered?" the vendor asked.

"Yes, to the rooms of Miss Hope in the Palace," I said.

"Wait a minute," the spoiled girl shrieked, "You are a commoner, and you dare insult me?"

"Apparently," I sighed. I did not look at the girl again. I simply motioned for Athena to follow me down the road, and the girl was too outraged to chase us.

"Who was that girl?" I asked. I could say something to Rowan, and maybe he could convince the girl's parents to encourage their daughter to leave Athena alone.

"She's just an arrogant bully," Athena said sullenly. "Will Dad really like the flowers, or did you just say that to antagonize her?"

"Of course, he will. Everyone likes flowers." I didn't mention that part of my motivation was to antagonize the girl, and hopefully get her to reconsider who should and should not get flowers. It was a small goal, but it was unlikely that anything I said would get that girl to reconsider the crueler comments she made about Athena's lack of a mother.

"Hope look at these daggers," Athena grabbed my hand and pulled me to a table filled with various blades.

"We can look, but you'll need to do your weapon shopping with your father," I said firmly. I picked up a small, curved knife with a decorative, carved handle. The blade was functional, so this clearly was not just a decorative piece.

"But look at the daggers! These ones are the same size as my practice ones," Athena pressed.

"Athena," I said firmly. "I will not get in trouble for buying you daggers. If your dad thinks you are ready to own real daggers, you can bring him down to the market and the two of you can make that choice together." I held out the knife. "I'd like to purchase this, for me."

"Weapons have to be delivered, not carried around the market," the vendor said.

That worked fine for me. "Have it sent to Miss Hope's rooms at the palace," I said as I held out my medallion.

He took the knife, then scanned my medallion for the payment. He took a beautiful wood box out from under the table and placed the knife in the recess created for it.

"You passed my test," Athena said as we walked away from the weapon display.

"Oh?" I teased. I suspected she was only pretending a test was her objective, and she would have said nothing if I had caved and bought the daggers for her.

"I convinced someone to purchase my first real set of daggers when I was seven, and right now I have four sets, all in Dad's armory. I convince the women who want to impress Dad to get them for me, then Dad takes them away. He says I can have them when I'm older."

"You convinced someone to buy you real weapons when you were seven?" I asked, both sickened and impressed.

"Some women will do anything to marry Dad," she said solemnly.

"Apparently," I said sarcastically. Privately, I wondered how serious those women were if they thought giving Athena weapons when she was too young to fully understand their danger was a viable way to gain Rowan's affection. It seemed more like an effective way to ensure he refused to marry them.

Next to the stall with weapons were several tables of clothing, mostly garish colors, and shirts with obnoxious slogans. Since Athena showed no interest in the clothing, and I thought the selection was ugly, we walked past those tables without slowing. The food carts, however, were another matter entirely. I smelled the savory aroma of meat cooked in sauces and the citrus smell of tropical fruit. Athena showed similar interest in the food, so we stopped and found the meat I wanted, and a seafood platter for Athena. As we ate, we continued on a leisurely pace through the section of the market that sold nick knacks and paintings, stopping to admire the most unusual items.

Athena found a set of simple cufflinks for Rowan, to go with the flowers, as she was quick to assure me. After that she lost interest in shopping, so we slowly made our way back to the building. Athena carried the cufflinks, everything else would be delivered to my room in the morning.

Athena went straight to her room, I assumed to go to sleep after that fun little trip. I was not so fortunate.

Rowan was waiting for me in the main sitting room, and Tatsu was gone.

"What did Tatsu want to talk to you about?" I asked. I took a seat across from him and grabbed a decorative pillow to hold in my lap as a physical barrier between us. It was both a comfort and a precaution.

"That's why I waited to talk to you. It seems he overheard two guards talking about you, he followed them and eavesdropped on their conversation."

"And that was an issue he wanted to share with you and not me because?" I prompted, a little put out that Tatsu's first response to hearing gossip about me was to gossip to Rowan about what he learned.

Rowan sighed loudly and glanced at the wall. Apparently, it was easier than looking at me. "Hope, are you aware your mother is the Queen of Talaraine?"

"Excuse me, my mother is what?" I demanded. I knew my mother was on Talaraine, and both Blaze and Millenia thought she would be easy to find, but no one mentioned she was the leader of an entire planet! It was rare for one person to have control of an entire planet, unless it was sparsely populated like Nexa. The Amaranth Empire was unusual because one person ruled over several planets, but I figured that position was more ceremonial than effective.

"On Karabeeya, she's called the Twice Royal Queen. Her own people refer to her as the Warrior Queen or the Protector Queen. Apparently, she's the illegitimate daughter of the former Queen of Talaraine and Prince Setne of the Royal House of Deva."

I scratched my nose. It made sense that my mother was Setne's daughter, why else would he have let me into his family? He wasn't exactly the sentimental type.

"I didn't know," I said as soon as I could speak with some semblance of calm. "How did those guards manage to find out?"

Rowan glanced at me. I didn't need to be an empath to see his discomfort and pain.

"Rowan?" I pressed.

"They managed to read your medical file, including your DNA test."

I glared at him, clutching the pillow tighter. "How long have you known the Queen of Talaraine was my mother?"

"The entire time I've known you," Rowan admitted. "Your DNA identified you as a bloodline descendant of the Houses of Deva, Aphelion, Paxa, and Summer. That particular combination can only be one of Queen Juliet's daughters, and you are the right age to be the missing twin. She had twins on Nexa, but only brought one child to Talaraine, the other was officially declared dead.

I bit my lip, to give myself a moment to think before I spoke. That moment didn't calm me down at all, and my tone was still harsh, but at least I didn't cry.

"Why couldn't you be bothered to tell me?"

"Until Tatsu relayed what he overheard, I thought you knew. I thought that was why you sought asylum here."

"When I sought asylum on Karabeeya, I wanted to work in the swamps. You were the one who convinced the king to let me stay with you. I couldn't figure out why you did that. Earlier today, after you kissed me, I thought your kindness was because you wanted a mistress."

The suggestion enraged Rowan, I saw the fury in his eyes. Good, that meant he felt some of what I did, some of that that helpless anger.

"I would never take a mistress, how dare you..."

"What then?" I interrupted. "Was I meant to be a fling before you settled down with a respectable bride? I guess mistress was aiming too high."

"Hope, an alliance with the Royal House of Talaraine," Rowan paused, and I realized his true aim.

"I was a pawn," I said. It was so much worse than a mistress. "I was a means to an end. You saw that I loved you and you knew you could use that. Well Surprise! I have no relationship, no real connection, with the Royal Family of Talaraine. They do not even know I'm alive, and if they did? I'm a traitor, a Nexan runaway who," I thought of Kayda. "I don't belong with any royal family, I'd be far too much of an embarrassment, a liability for my mother to claim." I tossed the pillow against the wall. The motion wasn't nearly as satisfying as I hoped. I stood up, not wanting to spend one more moment in the same room as Rowan.

"I'm out."

"Hope," Rowan stood and moved to follow me.

"Don't you dare," I snapped as I stepped to the door. "Please, just have enough respect for me to leave. Just give me that." I walked out of the room, through the hallway to the elevator.

As I rode the elevator back down to the ground floor, I realized I probably couldn't leave for good. If I were really some Talarainian princess, I could be captured and sent on the next ship to Talaraine, as a gesture of goodwill. It would be better for Valoria than letting me leave and losing the advantage of a possible alliance with Talaraine. No wonder Elle wanted me as her companion. I stayed close and developed a friendship with the Crown Princess of Valoria. A friendship that would aid Valoria politically.

As the doors opened to the ground floor, I realized whatever freedom I thought I gained when I left Nexa was just an illusion.

I was never more than a pawn.

# Chapter Eleven

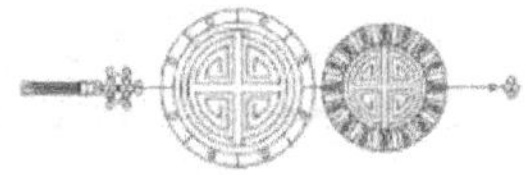

The market was still crowded, and more tables were in the process of being set up, with less family friendly displays. I stepped around a table offering classes on seduction and wondered if the food section still had something sweet still available. I was tired of running, I just wanted desserts and to find a room to rent for the night, somewhere where I could hole up and ugly cry for a few days. Having a goal, as pathetic as it was, I began to walk in the direction of the food stalls.

A small pebble struck my arm. I glanced in the direction it came from and saw Tatsu frantically waving me over to where he stood next to an empty stall.

Perfect, I could yell at him, demand to know why he told Rowan about the gossiping guards, instead of coming to me. I ran to where he hid. As soon as I reached him, he grabbed my arm. I felt like every inch of my skin tingled with uncomfortable numbness, then it faded away and I was fine.

"What did you just do?" I hissed.

"Quiet!" Tatsu whispered. "Did Rowan tell you what I heard?"

I nodded, speaking carried too much risk of shouting.

"The guards I told Rowan about are just over there. My invisibility charm doesn't mask sound, and I need to keep a hold of you for it to cover you too."

"Invisibility charm?" I demanded, just barely keeping my voice as quiet as his.

"How do you think I got in the city? Come on, they're moving."

I walked with Tatsu, curious despite my anger. We wove through the crowd, despite the fact that I could see myself and Tatsu, the crowds were completely unaware of us, making following the two men Tatsu focused on difficult.

The men we were following were not dressed as guards, and I did not recognize them, but it wasn't completely impossible that I had seen them in the building, and they left no impression at all.

At first, I thought they were just perusing the market, but after no spending more than a few seconds at the tables they stopped out, not long enough to look at anything, I began to suspect otherwise. They slipped behind a table, and we followed, careful not to get close enough for them to notice our footsteps. They wove through two alleyways, then slipped through a gap between two huge doors into a warehouse. At that point, I had moderately calmed down, enough to give Tatsu a temporary pass on confronting him about his conversation with Rowan. At the moment, this was more interesting, and a welcome distraction.

The two guards met with three others, a tall man, a short man, and an incredibly angry woman.

"Well?" the short man demanded.

"We confirmed it. The prince arrived back at the palace alone. He doesn't suspect anything amiss," one of the guards said.

"And the friend the princess was meeting?" the tall man asked.

"She's not one of ours. We merely gave her appropriate incentive to lure the princess away from her husband. One of my men is waiting in her home. It's such a tragedy when a beautiful young socialite walks in on a burglary and is killed by the thief. There have been so many break ins in that neighborhood. It truly is no surprise that someone was finally unlucky enough to catch them in the act," the guard said smugly.

"Just make sure nothing can be traced back to us. We need time to get the princess out of the city," the short man said.

"She's already out of the city," the other guard said. "We didn't take any chances. We injected her with a sedative and smuggled her out under bags of trinkets for the festival in the nearby cities. She'll be halfway to the coast by now. We're going to meet our contact at the boat, we just wanted to make sure we got paid before we continue to the next stage of the plan."

"Wise," the short man said coyly. "Bringing the princess here may have tempted us to kill her here and leave you with nothing more than a dead body, whereas if you don't get paid, she lives."

"We're loyal to the cause, we just need to eat," the guard said smoothly.

I grabbed at my pocket and realized too late that my screen was in my purse, in Rowan's main sitting room.

The tall man handed each guard a small bag. Once they were satisfied with the contents, they left, and we followed immediately behind them. Anyhow that we could contact the palace before they traveled too far was gone when they climbed into a flatbed truck.

Tatsu and I did not need to converse to know we were climbing onto the flatbed of the truck as they climbed into the cab. We laid flat, careful to keep a hold of each other, and the bars on the sides of the flat bed. The building was in the center of the city, but neither of us were willing to risk jumping off the vehicle to alert the city's law enforcement. What if the guards responded by sending a message to have Elle killed immediately? What if she was already dead?

When they passed through the wall, I realized there was one thing I hadn't considered, the cursed rain. It was pouring, cold, and the worst part was it was likely creating the same effect on us that it did on the dome, creating two little people shaped voids for the water to run off of. Still, it was dark, and they weren't looking at the back of their vehicle, so with grim determination, neither of us spoke, and we bared the cold in stoic silence, each waiting for our good luck to run out.

It felt like an eternity before we reached the harbor. The journey certainly took far longer than the drive had been with Rowan, in his nice warm, dry car.

When we finally reached the harbor, we drove onto a pier that unlike several others, lacked the party atmosphere as the celebrations of the Fertility Festival began a little early. As soon as the guards were out of the cab, a woman approached them.

"What's wrong with the back of your truck?" she yelled.

"Find Elle, I'll distract them," I hissed as close to Tatsu's ear as I could. He nodded and squeezed my hand quickly before he let me go.

Judging from the reactions of the guards and the woman, I was suddenly visible again. Lucky for me, the stupid fools did not have guns readily available. I grabbed my staff and twisted it, so it shot to full size as I jumped off the truck. I swung the staff as soon as I hit the ground. The momentum of the swing and the fact that the guard didn't move nearly fast enough gave me a lucky hit. He went down, and he probably sustained severe enough head trauma to stay out of the fight.

The second guard tried to get back in the cab, likely there was a weapon there, so I picked up a pebble, charged it, and threw it over the cab. It exploded near the guard throwing him away from the truck and dazing him.

"Hope, I got her!" Tatsu yelled.

I turned around and saw a distortion in the rain move towards the cab.

"Can you drive?" I asked, staring at the distortion. It was hard to tell exactly, but it looked like Tatsu was carrying Elle over his shoulder. She was hurt, if not worse, and he held a wig in his hand.

"When would I have learned to drive?" Tatsu demanded.

"Right. Passenger side," I directed as I ran around the truck to the driver's side.  I struck the guard on my way; the idiot was struggling to his feet when he really should have stayed down and twisted my staff, so it shrank to the smaller size.

I climbed into the cab and checked on Elle and Tatsu in the back. Elle was pale, likely drugged, and didn't seem injured, although either she had been wearing a wig the entire time, I knew her, or her kidnappers shaved her head and dyed the stubble a dull brown. I turned back to the immediate task at hand. Driving. I had seen Rowan drive once, but usually I was in the back of a vehicle, not paying attention to the driver.

Fortunately, this wasn't nearly as complicated as Rowan's car. There were only two pedals on the floor and not nearly as many buttons on the steering wheel and dashboard. I took that to mean at least some of the options were either automated or nonexistent.

I started the truck, put it in reverse, turned to watch behind me, and saw three vehicles converging on the pier. No problem, if I quickly backed up on the main road, I could avoid them all and could possibly get ahead. I pressed my foot down hard on the gas pedal.

And drove straight onto the boat in front of the truck.

I slammed my foot on the brake too late, and I struck my head against the steering wheel.

"What was that?" Tatsu demanded.

I pressed my hand against my head. My neck hurt nearly as much, but only my forehead was bleeding.

"I don't know how to drive either." I grunted. I took a deep breath and focused my healing magic on the cut and sore muscles. The euphoria returned. Rather than shy away from it, I clung to it, knowing that when it faded, I could lose control of my telepathy again.

"Hope," Tatsu said as people climbed through the wreckage of the boat and out of the vehicles on the pier.

There were too many people and there was no way to escape while protecting Elle.

# Chapter Twelve

I looked around. This time our opponents had guns, and they were ready. From their grim determination and fatalistic resolves, I realized they were willing to gun down their own and be killed in turn, as long as they succeeded in killing us.

"Hope, what do we do?" Tatsu asked tentatively.

I shook my head. Surrender wasn't even an option, they wanted Elle dead.

While I was frozen, indecisive, the boat started to rock. I gripped the steering wheel. The boat capsizing wouldn't be much better, I was still a poor swimmer and didn't want to go back in the freezing water.

Before the boat capsized, a huge wave splashed over the boat and a huge blue head shot out of the water.

I had seen the carvings through the building of dragons, but I wasn't prepared for the size of a sea dragon. Its head was the size of the truck. It snarled down at everyone on the boat, and I got a disconcerting view of its enormous, jagged sharp teeth, some of with were as long as my forearm.

*Hope don't touch any metal in your vehicle.*

I knew the telepathic presence, although it shouldn't have been possible for Rowan to communicate through my mental wall.

"Tatsu, make sure you and Elle aren't touching metal," I said quickly.

The dragon didn't give us much time to comply before it roared.

The sound was loud and accompanied by the crack of thunder and flashes of blinding light. I covered my eyes with my hands and flinched from the echoing thunder and screams.

In less than a minute, it was silent. I moved my hands and looked around. Those who had surrounded us laid on the ground, most didn't move, and those who did only twitched a limb. They were all burned from the lightning storm.

The dragon glared at me through the windshield, then disappeared back into the ocean.

"Looks like the Elite Guard just showed up," Tatsu commented.

"Are you alright?" I asked.

"I didn't know Dragons could get that big. Who was that?"

"Rowan," I guessed. I climbed out of the truck and stepped over the blistered remains of the tall man I had seen earlier in the warehouse. I was careful not to breathe through my nose, I'd smelled the burned dead before, and was quick to minimize a repeat of the experience.

"Hope!" Alistair shouted. He waved from the pier. "Who's with you?"

"Tatsu and Princess Estelle. She needs medical attention, they drugged her and I'm not good at correcting chemical imbalance," I shouted back.

With shocking efficiency, Alistair arranged for healers to get Elle out of the wreckage and sent back to the city. Tatsu volunteered to give the guards a detailed account of what happened, freeing me to join Alistair at the end of the pier.

"How did you know where we were?" I asked. I followed his gaze to the choppy waves of the harbor.

"Your medallion flagged when it passed out of the city limits. Rowan was worried, but he also wanted to give you space. When he realized you were in danger, he called us and went into the ocean." Alistair frowned and knelt on the edge of the pier.

"There he is. The idiot. We could have taken care of those imbeciles without his theatrics."

Rowan swam to the surface, slowly. He looked sick. When his head broke the surface, Alistair grabbed his arm and pulled him out of the water in a quick motion that revealed his freakish strength.

Alistair handed Rowan a towel out of his bag. Rowan closed his eyes, then sat up. I looked away, not wanting to get caught staring at Rowan, no matter how attractive he was, or how he still affected me, even when I was angry.

"Thorne, do you have any runner's gum?" Rowan asked.

"If you eat runner's gum now, you'll really pay for it later," Alistair warned.

"I know," Rowan said.

Alistair handed him the bag. "Side pocket." He gently put his hand on my shoulder and guided me away. "Let's give him a minute to get dressed."

Rowan joined us sooner than I anticipated. He had an almost jittery energy, the runners gum gave a temporary energy boost, but it came at the cost of a harsher crash once the effect wore off.

"Hope, I need to talk to you, privately," Rowan said.

I nearly refused, I had no desire to listen to his excuses or justifications, but Rowan had just saved my life, the very least I could do was honor this request.

Rowan took me to one of the guard vehicles and we climbed into the back seat. It wasn't complete privacy, but it was better than nothing, and it would be best for Rowan if he was sitting when the gum wore off, best still if he was sitting in a vehicle so no one would have to move him when the guards were ready to leave.

"Hope, did Tatsu tell you the rest of what he heard from the guards that were talking about you?" Rowan asked.

"Oh, there's more?" I snapped. "Let me guess, some other tidbit that makes me more valuable to Karabeeya?"

"Hope, please let me speak. There's something you need to know."

I folded my arms across my chest, and leaned against the door, as far from him as I could get, and glared impatiently.

He took a deep breath and ran his fingers through his hair, ruffling his damp hair and being completely unfair in how much more attractive that simple motion made him.

"They didn't just talk about you being a princess of Talaraine. They also mentioned a woman, Megaera, was searching for you. She had a bounty for your capture and a smaller bounty for information on your location. They were debating which bounty they wanted, the risk-free option of just exposing your location, or the greater reward of capturing you and delivering you to this woman."

I bit my lip and tensed against the door. Megaera was my grandmother, and the woman who used telepathy to force me to do unspeakable things.

"Hope, they decided to reveal your location. We aren't sure if they message was sent our not."

"I should have killed them on the pier," I whispered. Were they among the injured and dead the Elite Guard were moving off the boat? Or had they escaped?

"I don't know that it would have made a difference. For all we know, the message has already been sent."

I couldn't get any closer to the door, and the vehicle was unlikely to swallow me up and keep me safe from the ramifications of what Rowan was telling me. Megaera was coming for me, and considering how sporadic my powers had been lately, I couldn't hide from her forever. I ran my tongue over my teeth, grateful they were their proper shape.

"Hope, I have a plan. I know how to keep her from hurting you." He rested his hands on my shoulders, a gentle offer of a hug, but I shook my head and stayed against the door.

"I have to run," I whispered. I couldn't escape her forever, but I could stop her from going after Rowan and Athena. Although history said otherwise. What would stop those guards from telling her about the family that took me in and protected me?

"Hope, she's never going to stop looking, and your telepathy is growing, she'll find you that way if nothing else."

I flinched. It was worse to hear Rowan had made the same realization I had.

"But... if you are part of a powerful House, she'll have no chance of getting to you. If you were part of a strong enough House, she won't risk it. Nexa doesn't have resources to go to war with everyone, they'll risk annihilation."

I glared at him. I couldn't go to Talaraine and beg my mother to welcome me into her family. There was no way a Queen would want to acknowledge kinship with someone like me.

"Hope," he whispered. He leaned in closer, this time, hesitantly, I accepted his embrace. Call it weakness, or a demonstration of how pathetic I really was, but I felt safe in his arms, even if he did smell like salt water.

"I wasn't kidding before. I'm not ready to go to Talaraine. They think their daughter is dead. It's best for them to keep thinking it, rather than know my past," I whispered weakly.

"You have my word, the Royal House of Talaraine won't find out about you, unless you make the choice to tell them of your own free will," he murmured into my hair. "I wasn't talking about the House of Talaraine. I was talking about the House of Argentia."

I pulled away from him then. Self-preservation was more tempting than political gain, but no less painful. Was it so horrible to want Rowan to love me as much as I loved him?

"So instead of wanting to marry me for political gain, you want to marry me so you can protect me? It's not... I don't want your pity," I whispered. I glanced at the door handle. Running was such a tempting option.

Rowan took a slow, deep breath and closed his eyes. "I'm lowering my mental wall. Ask me anything."

I shifted. To read his emotions, I would have to lower my own wall, and he would know exactly how I felt. I rested my head against the cold glass window, unable to look at him as I risked the fallout of that exposure.

Lowering my wall was hard, but I was rewarded with the overwhelming strength of his love, tempered only with frustration and fear.

"Will you tell Talaraine about me?" I started. Best get the question that created this divide out of the way first.

"No."

"Will the royal family?"

"No. Remy didn't support that plan to begin with, and the King trusts me. I can and I will convince them not to reveal your identity to Talaraine."

I nearly cut him off, but there was one more question. "Do you have any other motivation for marrying me, besides protecting me from Megaera?"

Fear, hesitation, then desire. This was overwhelming! I couldn't tell if he was reacting to my attraction or if I was reacting to his.

"Yes," he said finally.

I looked sharply at him and tensed, ready to push him away and flee the vehicle.

"I want to marry you because I love you. I have loved you since the day I first saw you and it terrified me to care so much, to want so much. I want you to be part of my life, every day. I want to hear your laugh and your unexpected comments. I want you to surprise me every day, and every day I want to be worthy of your trust, your love. I want you to be part of Athena's life, and the mother of her sibling. I want you to be part of my family and..."

He may have had more to say, but I interrupted him with a kiss more passionate, more mind numbing than the one we shared before. I ran my fingers through his hair as he trailed kisses down my cheek, jawline, then neck.

"Rowan," I gasped as he found an extremely sensitive patch of skin just under my ear.

He responded by kissing the side of my mouth. I gently pressed my mouth against his lower lip as I grabbed at his shirt and tugged it.

That jarred him. He grabbed my hand, his grip firm but not painful.

"Uh, we are in a car, with windows," he grumbled. He pulled

away from me and I sat up, breathless.

Rowan glanced at me. "You didn't actually answer my question."

I risked scooting over to his side of the car and took a deep breath as I reinforced my mental wall, leaving me with only my own emotions, desire, and attraction. I sat in his lap and rested my head against his shoulder. Starting to make out may have been a reckless choice, but I wanted to stay close to him, to feel him breathe.

"I'll marry you," I said as he held me close. "But we need to work on our communication."

"It would have been ideal to have a greater chance to get to know each other before the marriage," he admitted. "As they do in the general population, but if Megaera received that message…"

I nodded. "The sooner the better, but I call dibs on the six month-long retreat. Athena can come for part of it, but I want you without the distractions of the Court for a little while, even if we can't take the time right away, or all at once."

"Agreed," Rowan said. He kissed that sensitive spot under my ear again, just to torment me, then rested his head back in the space between the seat and the window.

"Are you alright?" I asked. I could tell the runners gum was wearing off, and fast.

"Hmm," he said noncommittally. He closed his eyes, and I rested my head against his shoulder as he relaxed.

When Alistair opened the driver's door, I was the only one who startled awake.

"We're ready," Alistair announced. He climbed into the car and turned it on before glancing back at me and Rowan.

"I thought you two were arguing."

I shook my head and rested against Rowan.

There was still so much to fear in the future, but at least I would not have to face it alone.

# Books By This Author

**Dragon's Sacrifice**

The sequel to Dragon's Gambit

**Dragon's Soulmate**

The events of Dragon's Sacrifice, from Phoenix's point of view.

**Dragon's Loyalty**

An early look at the final book in the Palingenesis Trilogy. Dragon's Loyalty will be available in ebook format in 2022

**Sapphire Marionette**

**Mars Diamond**

**Finding Topaz**

Coming Soon as an ebook titled Topaz Royalty

**Autumn Phoenix**